Antithesis of
Supremacy

Adrian Johnson

ISBN: 978-1-963949-90-2 (Paperback)

ISBN: 978-1-963949-91-9 (Hardcover)

Printed in the United States of America

Contents

Chapter 1 The Nation's Cry Turn To Tragedy...................................1

Chapter 2 Uncover The Books...13

Chapter 3 The Wise Mentor...24

Chapter 4 The Demand For A New Leader.....................................32

Chapter 5 The War Of Two Nations...39

Chapter 6 Revelation Of Betrayal..50

Chapter 7 The Temptation Of Power..60

Chapter 8 Road To Redemption 79

Chapter 9 Inner Struggle...96

Chapter 10 Embracing The Legacy 112

Chapter 1
The Nation's Cry Turn To Tragedy

Dawn's light bathed the towering structures of Washington, DC, casting a radiant blessing upon the city's awakening skyline. The early morning sun painted the rooftops with hues of warmth, infusing the urban landscape with a sense of renewed vitality. As the city came to life, the sunlight bounced and reflected off from the glass and steel of the buildings while softly brushing against historical monuments. It was the sight of brilliance that welcomed the promise of a new day.

Washington sprawled before him, a tapestry of life woven through time. President Thomas' steps echoed in the cobblestone streets, carrying him towards the heart of a metropolis' secrets whispered in every shadow. His gaze, a blend of determination and contemplation, swept across the bustling scene. The morning air was filled with the aroma of fir trees and freshly cut grass. It mixed with his own smell of cedarwood cologne, polished leathers from his dress boots, and the musky odor of the smell of the hair wax that slicked his hair back. The only other thing that the air carried was the hum of fervent voices.

Change was in the air, an undercurrent of unrest that tugged at the heart of the city. For decades, greed and power ruled the land. Powerful figures seized positions of power and subjected their people to a reign of corruption and oppression. America had withered under their rule, its potential stifled, its promise eclipsed by shadows cast by those who cared only for their own gain. At the heart of it all was an ancient text that allowed these shadowy figures to rule over the country.

1

Of course, the unrest was impossible to contain. While powerful figures exercised their rule without remorse or empathy, it left hatred and desperate hope for change with the common man.

The city square had become a symbol of defiance. It was a place where the echoes of powerful protests reverberated through the years. They held banners bearing passionate slogans. It happened so frequently that it had basically become a tradition. Of course, over time, some of the crowd had thinned, and the placards weathered, their colors fading but their messages enduring. Still, when people would pass a certain age, they would be replaced by the young. The nation had been gripped by a relentless demand for change, a collective outcry against the era of greed and power struggles that had plunged the country into corruption.

But today…today was different. In the heart of the square, people stood as steadfast participants in this ongoing movement of change. Their eyes, once ablaze with anger and hope, had mellowed into a determined gaze that reflected years of unwavering commitment. The air had held a sense of both weariness and resilience, the atmosphere charged with the weight of battles fought and battles yet to come.

As of the past six months, tensions between the US and Russia had escalated to new heights. With the latter threatening to push for war through means of mass destruction, the US had been aiming for a peaceful resolution to smooth things over.

Unfortunately, the threat had been looming for a long while since. The source of the conflict was a direct result of a mining contract that would allow Russia to mine oil from Diomede Island off the coast of Alaska. The island, although smack dab in the middle of the two countries, had legally been a part of Alaska, and by extension, the United States. However, a private Russian mining company—that was secretly a subsidiary of the Russian Government—managed to secure mining rights under the guise of foreign investment, spurring a big debate over whether it was a way to enact state-sponsored surveillance or cause a systematic depletion of resources.

Back home in the States, the reception was mixed. Some saw it as an act of foreign investment and a sign of good things to come. They saw brightened economic prospects and a chance for a better life for themselves and their children. Others, of course, saw it as a form of aggression, to deprive the people of the US and its land of natural resources and a covert act of war.

With all this going on, Russia had been secretly planning conflicts with other small nations in its vicinity. Some people had suspected that the whole operation was a cover-up, a way to keep major world powers like the US busy so they couldn't intervene. The tensions between the groups that advocated for and against the mining operations were palpable. Someone had to do something about it, and President Thomas had decided that he was going to be that someone.

The imposing structure of the Presidential Palace loomed ahead. Its magnificence was juxtaposed against the turmoil brewing outside. President Thomas walked up the steps of the building. On a quiet day, his wing tip Derbys would have clacked against the marble steps, producing a distinct echo throughout. But on a day like this, with the raised sounds from the crowd, a barrage of questions from reporters, and his secret service surrounding him, he couldn't hear a thing.

Since his election just three years ago, President Thomas had become a figure that was beloved by the masses. People admired him; they respected him. And most of all, they had a firm belief that he represented hope—the hope of change. On this day, he was determined to do just that. He wanted to be able to bridge the gap between the two groups and uphold harmony among the masses.

President Thomas wanted to be the one to broker peace between the Russians and one of their neighboring territories. He stood at the face of a negotiation that could determine their nation's destiny and in turn, his own. The people had seen his tireless efforts to bridge the gap between factions with clashing ideologies, and they understood the weight of his burden.

With a deep breath, he entered the Presidential Palace. President Thomas had always felt drawn to its beating heart, the place where history and modernity converged like the threads of a complex web. He had been to the building on several occasions for some purpose or another. This was also the place where he would take his son, Thomas, whenever he had matters to attend to.

This morning, however, the President was by himself. He woke up early, kissed his wife, said his goodbyes to his sons, and got into the black, tinted Chevrolet Suburban that was waiting for him. After months of negotiations, he had finally convinced Boris Khrushchev, the Russian President, to agree to appear at a videoconference with him. President Thomas hoped that this would signal the start of what would eventually lead to the end of any nefarious plans for war. President Thomas cared about his people, but more than that, he cared about having peace instituted throughout his land.

"Good afternoon, President Khrushchev," President Thomas began, his tone measured and respectful, bearing the echoes of countless conversations and negotiations.

"Good afternoon, President Thomas," Khrushchev responded, his voice carrying a slight hint of formality. President Thomas sensed that although he had come face to face with him, Khrushchev was still a bit hesistant. Still, behind the layers of political discourse, they both understood the gravity of the moment. He had to.

"We've come a long way," President Thomas said, trying to soften his way into getting Khrushchev to open up. President Thomas' gaze was unwavering as it met the pixelated representation

4

of the Russian President. "Months of deliberations, negotiations, and sleepless nights."

Khrushchev nodded, his expression softening just slightly. "Indeed, we have. Especially the sleepless nights. My wife resents you for that," he replied with a muffled laugh.

President Thomas leaned forward slightly, his hands resting on the table before him. "But we're here today, Mr. Khrushchev, because we recognize the stakes. Our nations, our people, they deserve better than the threat of conflict, the specter of war."

Khrushchev's eyes met President Thomas's, and there was a flicker of understanding between them. "I agree, President Thomas. We are stewards of the future. I know you are beloved by your people, as am I. They may love us in different ways, but it is all a result of the decisions we make for their benefit."

Unsure of what he hinted at, President Thomas stayed firm as he continued. "Mr. Khrushchev," he said, his voice deep as it echoed throughout the room, "we have the power to shift the narrative, to steer our nations toward a future where cooperation and understanding prevail. The decisions we make in this moment will resonate for generations to come."

Khrushchev's gaze remained fixed on President Thomas, his expression introspective and calculating. "You are right, President Thomas. It is not only about our terms and treaties; it is about shaping the legacy of our leadership. I, for one, am bound to mine."

"I'm glad to hear it, President Khrushchev," President Thomas replied. "Your administrative secretary mentioned something about finalizing the plans at the border?"

"Ah, yes, President Thomas. It will be a symbolic gesture to the people, don't you think? I will have lunch ready for you at arrival. We can talk about peace and the future of our nations as we…wine and dine…?" President Khrushchev said.

"Very well, President Khrushchev, I will have Airforce One on standby, and I can get there within five hours if the weather holds."

"See you then, Mr. President. *Dosvidaniya*."

With that, the screen turned off, and President Khrushchev disappeared from view, leaving President Thomas to look at his own reflection. President Thomas straightened his blazer and pulled out his phone, and started dialing.

"Hey Avienda, I won't be coming home for a while. I'm going to Russia. Tell the kids I love them."

***

Airforce One touched down at the military landing strip on the Novograd border. The air was frigid and dry, cast over by fog. On the ground, a few layers of mud and ice had mixed in with each other making it hard to step foot on the ground without the possibility of slipping over. The Russian military stood alert near the runaway and at the entrance to the border. A few soldiers hung around aimlessly, looking in random directions or sitting by idly. It seemed like they were all set for the President's arrival.

Of course, President Thomas hadn't come empty-handed either. Trailing behind his plane, there were two F-16 fighters, all in formation, piloted by some of the best that the USAF had to offer. And behind them, there were four Black Hawk Helicopters with Marines and Special Ops personnel. They were the first to land, with all the personnel scattering around to secure the area. Shortly afterward, Airforce One touched down on the runway and came to a stop.

The ladder extended out from the plane, and President Thomas took some steps and descended down. As soon as he did, a huddle of Russian soldiers approached the plane. At the center of them, Khruschev stood, smoking a cigar and tapping the smoke from the end of it. He wore a thick woolen jacket with a fur collar that periodically swayed in the harsh winds as well as a big hat with ear muffs that covered his head.

Once President Thomas started descending from the plane, his nerves began to fray. He couldn't shake off the feeling that something was amiss. Not really knowing what else to think, he ignored it, chalking it up to the cold weather and continued his descent down.

The troops for both countries stood at a distance as their leaders met with each other to discuss terms. President Khrushchev emerged from the huddle, his presence commanding and formidable. President Thomas put on a diplomatic smile, extending his hand in greeting. Khrushchev extended his own hand and shook it; his grip was firm, but there was a chilling coldness in his eyes that sent a shiver down President Thomas' spine.

"I hope this meeting signifies a new chapter in the U.S.-Russia relations," President Thomas said, his voice steady despite the rising apprehension within him, "one of collaboration and understanding,"

"Indeed, President Thomas. We have much to discuss." Khrushchev's smile was thin, almost mocking, as he responded. "Please, come, sit."

The two presidents sat at the dinner table across from one another. The table was populated with all kinds of bread, cheeses, and meats. At the center of the table, there was a bottle of vodka with two glasses. Khruschev poured himself a drink before handing the other to President Thomas. As Khrushchev did all this, he had a casual and slightly unnerving smile plastered across his face.

President Thomas couldn't shake off the feeling that Khrushchev knew something he didn't. He pressed on, choosing to address the issue at hand. It was a delicate subject, one that had ignited conflicts and accusations between their nations in the past.

"I appreciate your assurance, President Khrushchev," Thomas said cautiously, "but actions speak louder than words. We've seen evidence of Russian interference in our democratic processes. We need tangible steps to rebuild trust."

Khrushchev's laughter filled the air, but it was devoid of warmth. It sent a chill down Thomas's spine, confirming his worst fears.

"Ah, political interference, a delicate subject, indeed," Khrushchev said, his voice dripping with sarcasm. "But I assure you, President Thomas, Russia is committed to international norms and cooperation."

President Thomas' suspicions intensified, but he tried to maintain his composure. He glanced at the exit, noting Khrushchev's advisors positioning themselves strategically, blocking any potential escape routes. Then, he saw that a large number of Russian soldiers emerged, far greater than there had initially been. It looked like they outnumbered the American soldiers 20 to 1. From the hills, Russian soldiers with sniper rifles and rocket launchers poked out. The trap was closing in.

"What is the meaning of this, President Khrushchev?" President Thomas asked, his voice trembling with a mix of anger and fear. "This meeting was supposed to be an opportunity for dialogue."

Khrushchev leaned closer, a smirk playing at the corner of his lips. "Dialogue, indeed. But sometimes, actions speak louder than words, President Thomas," he said, his voice laced with menace.

The realization struck Thomas like a bolt of lightning. He had walked into a carefully laid trap, one designed to expose the vulnerabilities of the United States and undermine its leadership on the world stage.

Desperation crept into Thomas's voice as he tried to reason with Khrushchev. "I implore you to think about the long-term consequences of your actions, President Khrushchev. Escalating tensions will only lead to further suffering and instability."

Khrushchev paused, momentarily considering President Thomas' words. The silence was suffocating, each heartbeat echoing louder than the last.

"Perhaps you're right, President Thomas," Khrushchev finally conceded with a sigh. "But remember what you said? This is not about single actions; this is about legacy. Your people stand behind you because you inspire them with hope. My people, however, they stand behind me because they admire me, because they think I am formidable and unbroken. The world is a fragile place, and the balance of power can shift swiftly. You can only rule when you have the strength to overpower weakness."

President Thomas looked around, frantically looking for a way out as his breaths became labored. He saw his soldiers raise their guns to try to protect them, but it was no use. There were simply too many Russian soldiers present.

"...and weakness, I shall crush," President Khrushchev said as he raised his hand, commanding his men to attack.

In one instant, a flurry of bullets sprayed in all directions. The smell of gunpowder and blood filled the air. Despite being able to secure a few casualties of their own, the American soldiers were ruthlessly gunned down. Flashes of muzzle fire illuminated the bloody faces of soldiers as they dropped to the ground. No matter how hard they tried to survive, it was no use. They were surrounded by the Russian military in open space with no cover. Soldier after soldier fell to the ground, emptying the crimson contents of their life.

After the entire force was gunned down, President Thomas was the last to still be standing. He had been mortally wounded and instinctually put his hand over his stomach. His suit had been bloodied completely, and his bulletproof vest was no match for the barrage of fire that chewed through him. With a limp, he tried to make his way to President Khrushchev, still bleeding out of his mouth.

Khrushchev looked at the sight and laughed maniacally. He pulled out his phone and started recording the stumbling President. "Oh…what a pity," he said before turning the camera back to himself. "This. This is what happens when weakness inhabits the world. It is a plague, a curse. And…" he said, pulling a revolver out of his coat and turning the camera back to President Thomas, "…it must be eradicated."

Khrushchev pulled the trigger, sending a bullet through President Thomas' head and sending him to the ground with a spray of blood.

***

The aftermath of the incident sent shockwaves throughout the world. The world stood in disbelief at the mere inhumanity of how President Thomas had been killed. Khrushchev had sent the assassination video out as a message to the rest of the world. He did not care about his or his country's public image. He placed his priorities on being able to continue to do whatever he wished with little to no intervention from the outside world.

Unfortunately, his plan worked.

None dared to intervene with Russia's plan to usurp control over the region. The extreme display of power had made him formidable on the world stage. And no one, not even the United States, dared to defy him.

Back home, news of the President's assassination had left the nation weeping. The beloved President had inspired many and left immense hope in the people. His death ultimately told his people one thing—no matter what, pure power and corruption were what won at the end of the day. While Khrushchev may have pulled the trigger, what really led him to be in front of the gun in the first place was the unfettered corruption and greed that occupied the higher office.

Jonathan, President Thomas' son, recognized this early on. He knew the real culprits to blame for his father's death were the people occupying government offices. They were the ones who accepted bribes and fell under the influence of the Russians in the first place. If it wasn't for their corruption, there wouldn't have been an invitation for foreign invasion into their country. And more than that, there wouldn't have been such a strong divide in the country itself. And if that was the case, his father would not have felt compelled to go to such lengths to fix the system.

No doubt, there were those that knew of President Thomas' fate yet did not care to warn him or intervene. In fact, they practically allowed it to happen. In their eyes, he was a liability. And by letting him die, they got two birds with one stone.

Inspired by his father's legacy and impassioned to continue through the injustice to do good for his country, Jonathan set forth to take over his father's position. Being a passionate political science student with a great sense of morality and lessons of a lifetime imparted to him by his father, he already had all the makings of a great leader.

Jonathan took office just a few years after his father's death. The entire nation cheered him on. They, too, wanted to see President Thomas' legacy live on, even if it was in the form of his son. He wanted to embody fairness and hope in his rule. He wanted to be the one to put an end to lawlessness in the highest office where dishonest gain and bribes rule.

Unfortunately, it all happened far too soon. The nation's desire to push past its sadness and inspire hope again meant that Jonathan had taken office far sooner than he would have. While his father had taught him a great deal about politics and the world, he still had much to learn.

Being overzealous and idealized meant that Jonathan was ruling without keeping a close eye over his allies and enemies. No matter how grand his plan of change was, he could not remove corruption and treachery from high office.

Those who benefitted from these ill means saw Jonathan as a threat, just as they had seen his father. When the time came, they wouldn't stand for his efforts to clean up the affairs in his country. Without a conscience, they lived easy lives, and they weren't about to let him take that away from them.

In a diplomatic campaign across the country, the young leader had disappeared overnight with no trace. It seemed he had all but vanished. In an investigation to find some trace of him, the FBI found Jonathan's body a few days later, stuffed into one of the maintenance tunnels of New York's subway system.

Chapter 2
Uncover The Books

The sun had dipped below the horizon, casting a warm, golden glow across the landscape. As the day gradually surrendered to the embrace of the evening, the world took on a different shade, painted in the colors of twilight. The sky transformed into a canvas of pastel pinks, purples, and deepening blues as if nature itself was putting on its own masterpiece.

In the quiet of the evening, the city's bustling streets began to wind down. The once hurried footsteps of pedestrians now moved at a relaxed pace, and the rhythm of life calmed down a little. Streetlights flickered to life, their gentle glow casting elongated shadows on the pavement.

Amid this transition from day to night, a small café at the corner of the street came alive with a cozy ambiance. The soft murmur of conversations, blended with the clinking of cutlery against plates, created a symphony. Inside, the aroma of freshly brewed coffee wafted through the air, intermingling with the faint scent of blooming flowers from a nearby garden.

Seated by the window, a lone figure gazed out at the changing scenery. She sipped her steaming cup of tea, feeling the warmth seep into her hands and soothe her thoughts. Her eyes wandered over the dusky streets, lost in thought as she typed away on her laptop in a race against the fading daylight.

Lina was a seasoned journalist who had worked for the Aurora Chronicle for over 15 years. She was always driven by journalistic integrity and the need to uncover the truth. Unfortunately, her career was cut short for this very reason. When she reported on a few scandals and acts of corruption in the higher offices of the government, it got her a lot of the wrong kind of attention. When that reflected back on the newspaper itself in terms of lack of support for funding and a tarnished reputation, they decided to let her go.

Now on her own, she decided to work independently. She had partnered up with a few other lone stragglers like herself to form an online publication that reported on events. This time, there were no names of the journalists attached to the articles. Everything was kept anonymous, so nothing bad could befall those who reported on the events.

Of course, those who were being reported on didn't take kindly to this kind of thing. But they knew they couldn't do much about the situation either. There were attempts by people holding high office to try and find where this publication was set up and who the faces behind it were. Thankfully, Lina and her cohorts managed to keep it a secret, whether it was by careful planning or sheer luck.

As the evening deepened, stars began to twinkle into existence, one by one, dotting the darkening canvas of the sky. The world outside seemed to hold its breath, suspended between day and night, past and present. And in that tranquil moment, anything seemed possible – the unraveling of secrets, the forging of new beginnings, and the quiet magic of the evening.

Lina's nose was buried in her screen. The light from her laptop reflected off her face and her thin-rimmed glasses. She went from email to email, document to document, trying to uncover some thread of connection between the scandal she was about to reveal. As she had long since suspected, things weren't ideal in high office. Officials collaborated and participated in all forms of corruption and malice to get ahead. And when some righteous figure came between them and their goals, they were silenced. Permanently.

Ever since President Thomas' death, the nation had wept and mourned the loss of an influential and beloved figure who led his country to its highest posts. But Lina looked at it another way. There was a lot about the events that didn't make sense to her. The way he was killed told her that it was planned and orchestrated in a much more elaborate way than it looked. Surely, this couldn't have been the result of just one entity, certainly not a single diplomatic official.

Granted, Khrushchev was evil. However, he was not foolish. Even someone like him understood the consequences that would entail him shooting the US president down in cold blood. What's worse, he did it in front of a camera while stating his intentions, all for the world to see. It just seemed a little too convenient. It played out like the plot of a movie with a clearly defined villain and hero. Lina's experience told her that things simply didn't work out that way in real life. She had always relied on her instincts in her career, and she knew for a fact that if something smelled fishy, then there was probably a good reason why.

Clearly, Khrushchev was not concerned about the wrath that the US would rain down on him, or the wrath of the world for that matter. This didn't make sense because he was a man of power, and he knew for a fact not to mess with a power greater than yours unless you had the means to match it.

So, what was the natural conclusion? Maybe he did have the means to match it. Maybe he had more power than he had let on. If he had no qualms about making himself out to be the villain, that meant he worked for something, or someone, greater than himself. It meant that he served someone even more powerful than him. And perhaps it was this kind of deal that allowed him to go around and do what he wished without any need to think about what kind of response would come.

So there she was, looking at a thousand different dead ends and pieces of information without having a clue of where it all led to. She had a hunch, she had a theory, and she had a few dozen scattered puzzle pieces. Now, all she had to do was put them all together and form the bigger picture. Lucky for her, this was something she had countless times before.

With a cock of her head and a drawn-out yawn, Lina glanced at her phone and put it face down on the table, then resumed typing away at her keyboard.

***

"Are you sure this source is legit?" Darien asked, looking at the article on his computer screen from all angles.

"Yeah, trust me. I got a hold of this site from a buddy of mine," Terrell replied as he sat down and took a sip from his energy drink.

Darien was President Thomas' younger son. He was the second in line after Jonathan. The President had made it so his two boys were raised on the same core values that he stood by. Jonathan tried to embody this in a very literal way when he tried to take up the mantle that his father had left for him. But unfortunately, things didn't turn out well for him.

With Jonathan unable to carry the torch, it was up to Darien to take over from where his brother had left things and try to move forward. While the rest of the world had moved on from his father's death, he hadn't. Darien didn't just want to be the next one in line; he wanted to understand why things had to happen the way they happened. Maybe if he could figure out what led to his brother's death, that would make it so he wouldn't find himself in the same situation.

Terrell was Darien's classmate and lifelong friend. He knew about Darien's ambition to rise to the top, to take up office where his father was and to rule the country with honor and integrity. He had supported his friend through this endeavor. They started out as teammates on the same high school football team and eventually grew closer the more they hung out in the presence of each other's

16

company. Darien knew he could trust Terrell to be there for him through thick and thin. He was more than a friend; he was like a brother.

When Terrell heard about President Thomas' death, he was devastated. There was, of course, the sadness he shared with the rest of the country on the passing of a wonderful leader. But beyond that, there was this underlying sadness he felt knowing his best friend's father had passed away.

After a few nights of hanging out at the skate park and sharing their sadness, they vowed to do something about it. They were not going to stand by idly while they saw the destruction of their country at the hands of those who claimed to look out for its best interests.

The first thing they decided to do was go back to the source— where all of this started in the first place. They knew this was greater than President Thomas or Khrushchev, greater than the conflict about the oil mining on Diomede Island. Even back then, as just a couple of teenagers, they had figured that this all stemmed from the one thing that everyone else seemed to overlook: the conflict between Russia and its bordering nation.

After months and months of digging around, tonight, they had found themselves looking at TruthStream, an independent online publication that posted the kind of news that other media outlets didn't. It offered key details into ongoing conflicts, details that no one seemed to know much about.

But it didn't seem like anyone was talking much about that site or even acknowledging its existence. In fact, no journalist bothered to follow up on the breadth of information the site laid out. Usually, they seemed to cannibalize each other like vultures, taking from each other's sources and cornering politicians with the scandals revealed about them. But here, it didn't seem like they knew, cared, or were forced to stay silent about what was going on.

17

"There's a lot here," Darien said as he backed away from the computer screen and slowly blinked his eyes.

"Oh yeah, and it gets much better," Terrell said, "I got a hold of someone that actually writes for the site."

"What? How? I thought it was anonymous?" Darien asked.

"It is," Terrell said as he finished his drink. "But…a friend of a friend got me in touch with her. She didn't want anything to do with us at first, but when I told her whose son you were, she seemed interested. She agreed to meet and share her findings with us. Some of them are unpublished."

"Alright. Seems promising," Darien replied as he looked away. "I mean, I've been reading this site for a while, and it looks like they're focusing on the conflict more than anything else. I think that's a pretty good sign right there."

"Yeah. I think we can learn a lot from her," Terrell said. "What about you? What did you find?"

"Oh, you're going to love this," Darien said as a piece of paper finished snaking its way out of the printer. It read, 'The Two Books.'

***

The moon hung like a silver pendant in the midnight sky, casting a soft glow over the quiet streets of the city. The air was cool and carried the promise of impending rain. The streets were nearly deserted, save for the occasional passing car that whispered through the damp asphalt.

In a tucked-away corner of the city, nestled between the towering buildings, stood a quaint coffee shop named "The Dark Roast." Its windows were fogged with warmth, a golden light spilling out onto the wet pavement, creating a cozy oasis in the midst of the urban night.

18

Darien and Terrell pulled up to the coffee shop. It sat in the heart of the town. Both of them emerged from their Ford Mustang and made their way inside, their footsteps echoing softly against the slick cobblestones.

Through the glass windows, they could see a few people inside the coffee shop. This time of night meant few people hung about unless they were your late-night workers, college students cramming in material for their test the next day, or…people that had something deep lingering on their mind.

At the back of the café, the two could see a lone figure engaged in her laptop and periodically sipping away at her coffee. She seemed like a woman with an air of quiet elegance, her movements deliberate and confident despite the late hour. Her dark hair cascaded down her shoulders like a waterfall of silk, and her eyes, though wary, held a glint of anticipation. She wore a long coat that swayed gently with the rhythm of the air conditioner above her; the collar turned up against the chill.

"I think that's her," Terrell said.

Darien nodded.

As if sensing their presence, Lina turned back and raised her hand, signaling to them. As she did, her chain bracelet slipped down her wrist and made its way towards the lower part of her arm.

Taking the cue, Darien and Terrell stepped into the café. The dimly lit brick-walled cafe was adorned with vintage posters and historic newspaper clippings. Darien and Terrell sat in their seats hunched over the small coffee table, engrossed in the scene before them. Their furrowed brows were illuminated by the lights that hung overhead, casting an atmosphere of intrigue as they pieced together the puzzle.

The table was adorned with a bunch of documents. One of them was obvious; it was the map that laid out Russia and its neighboring nations. The others included handwritten notes, some pictures, a

19

folder of official documentation, and an audio recorder with a few cassettes beside it.

Lina looked at Darien straight on as she studied his face carefully. Her presence commanded respect, a living archive of the nation's secrets. "The prodigal son, huh? You look so much like your father," she said. Then, with a frown, she continued, "Sorry for your loss. Both of them. It must be so hard to lose them in this pointless fight."

Darien's finger traced a line on the map connecting the two warring nations, each marked with a distinct emblem. He leaned back, his eyes meeting Terrell's, filled with a mix of determination and concern.

His voice was heavy with realization. "Thank you for saying that. I cared about them, but I also care about my country. I couldn't do anything to prevent their deaths. But I can find out who was responsible; I can find out how to restore America to its glory." He looked up to face her. "There's more to this conflict than meets the eye. These nations aren't just fighting over land and power. They're after something ancient and powerful," he said, looking at Terrell.

"The two books," Terrell said, "the Book of Truth and the Book of Ideology."

Lina raised her eyebrow and tilted her head sideways. "Books? What could books possibly have to do with all this chaos?"

Darien leaned in and lowered his voice. "These aren't ordinary books, Lina. Legends say that whoever possesses both books can reshape the destiny of nations. The Book of Truth is said to unveil the most guarded secrets, while the Book of Ideology holds the keys to influencing the masses."

Lina's eyes widened as she absorbed the weight of the revelation. Just then, her expression changed. It seemed like she had just come to a stark realization. She grabbed some of her handwritten notes and frantically flipped through the pages. She stopped on one particular page as her eyes darted back and forth, reading the material on them.

Finally, she dropped everything as she stared ahead with a blank expression. "Of course," she said.

"Are you okay?" Terrell asked.

"You've stumbled upon something really big. I didn't think it was anything important when I first read about them. I chalked it up to a stupid story or some kind of symbolism. But, you're right. The books you speak of have driven men to madness in their pursuit. I know exactly what you're talking about. In fact, it might just be the piece of the puzzle I needed to solve your father's death."

Darien and Terrell exchanged glances, surprised by her appearance. Lina's reputation preceded her – a relentless seeker of truth who navigated the treacherous waters of politics with an unwavering commitment.

With a curious look, Terrell said, "You seem to know more than the average journalist, Lina."

Taken aback by the comment, Lina took another sip of her coffee. "Oh, well, there's more to all of us than meets the eye. I've been reporting on this nation's political landscape for years, unearthing secrets that powerful men would rather keep buried. But then again, you aren't an average pair of boys, either. I would've never expected you to know so much."

Darien replied. "We've been following some leads for months. We don't know much about what's inside them. But we do know that there's an immense amount of power in each of them. Do you know where these books are?"

Lina smirked. "So, yes. I've been chasing whispers and breadcrumbs, and my trail has led me to believe that the books are hidden in the heart of the conflict itself. The question is, what do you plan to do with this knowledge, Darien?"

21

Darien's gaze hardened as he clenched his fist, determination burning in his eyes. "I won't let these books fall into the wrong hands, Lina. The consequences could be catastrophic," he said firmly.

Lina nodded. "Then you have my assistance. Uncovering the truth is what I do best, after all." She pushed some of her notes toward him. One of them contained a picture. "Recognize him?"

"Attorney Michael? He succeeded after my Dad," Darien replied.

"Exactly," Lina said. "It turns out he was in possession of the Book of Ideology. Remember how he was able to push laws without opposition and shape Congress? We all thought it was his charm, but really, it's the book."

"Interesting," Terrell replied.

"And," Lina said, "I'm sorry to have to say this, but this next part involves your Dad, and it's not great. Still wanna hear it?"

Darien looked at Terrell and sternly nodded his head. "Tell me."

Lina pushed another document to him. This time, it was a printout of a bunch of text messages between President Thomas and Attorney Michael.

'Michael, I know you have the damn book. You can hand it to me or else.'

'Or else what, Mr. President?'

'You don't know what you're dealing with. I'm the ruler of this nation. Only I should have the means for that level of power.'

'I'll ask again, Mr. President. Or else what?'

'Okay, Mr. Attorney, you've made your bed. I hope you can sleep soundly in it.'

"This happened a month before his death," Lina said. "He was on a campaign to discredit the Attorney, especially in the height of the negotiations. He wanted the book for himself and maybe even the power that came with it."

As Lina's words hung in the air, Darien and Terrell exchanged a perplexed glance. The pieces of the puzzle were slowly falling into place, revealing a web of intrigue they hadn't anticipated.

Darien murmured, his mind racing to connect the dots. "So, he was willing to manipulate political events to gain control over this powerful artifact."

Terrell nodded in agreement. "It seems like the President's ambitions got the better of him. But why didn't it work?"

Lina continued. "He was playing a dangerous game, especially against someone that had something as powerful as the Book of Ideology. I don't have a lot of evidence, but I do know that the Attorney might have been involved with the same entity that the Russian president was involved with. I guess you can imagine the rest. His plan failed, and he—"

"Died," Darien finished.

Lina nodded her head.

"Okay," Darien said as he looked at Terrell, giving him the cue to start heading back, "I think we're done here. Thank you for everything, Lina. We have a lot of work to do from here, but you helped us split some of the effort."

Lina smiled at them. "Glad to help you boys. Good luck. I hope you find what you're looking for."

Chapter 3
The Wise Mentor

Darien walked under the grey sky that had not changed for two days. It did not seem like it would rain, but the sky's color shed gloom all over the city. Darien sat on the patio overlooking the garden, the foam of his chair making him as comfortable as ever. His mind, however, was disturbed. It had been two days since he and Terrell had met Lina. And although things had begun to make sense, a lot was still there to uncover.

Darien stared at the long, uncut blades of the grass. It seemed less green than the previous day, probably because of the weather. He slightly tilted his head to his right as his complex thoughts took over once again. Darien scoffed. He was happy with thinking about grass.

Why did Michael have it? And even if he did, why was my Dad killed over it? And where does Jonathan fit into all of this? As these questions raced through Darien's mind, he heard a familiar sound approaching him. He recognized it in less than seconds. It was the muffled roar of Terrell's Mustang. The powerful V8 under the hood made its presence known from miles away. The car stopped some ten feet from where Darien was sitting. He didn't even look up.

Terrell got out of the car and slammed the door shut. Only he could be so cruel to such a car. Slamming car doors shut was Darien's pet peeve, and there was not a single instance where he had not yelled at Terrell for doing so, but today was different. Darien was too occupied with his thoughts to think about anything else. Terrell walked up to him immediately.

"You messaged?" Terrell skipped the greetings.

"Yeah." He pointed to another chair placed across from him. After several seconds, Darien spoke. "I didn't want to be alone."

Terrell nodded. It was his first time seeing grief in his friend's eyes. He knew this journey would not be easy and he was prepared for it. He could faintly hear some birds chirping in the distance. It was the only thing that somewhat seemed to lessen the gloominess of the setting.

"I'm here, brother. We'll figure it out together,' Terrell finally spoke. For some reason, he struggled to speak. His tongue did not seem to process the words coming out of his mouth. Maybe it was because of seeing Darien in this condition. Darien did not give up easily, but he seemed defeated, which scared Terrell. "There's so much left to uncover, Darien. You have to stay strong and determined," Terrell said, oblivious to how his friend would react.

Darien turned his head toward him and smiled. His words of encouragement seemed to have immediately worked. Darien got lost in thought for a while and then looked at his friend again.

"You're right. We can't let this get to either of us." Darien had always been implicitly grateful to Terrell. "What do you get by doing this?" Darien asked.

"What do you mean?"

"You know, my Dad got shot in front of the world. My brother was killed, in a mafia-like shooting. I want to know what happened to them. I want to connect the dots. I want to find the truth. What motivates you? Why have you stuck with me all this while?" Darien asked, immediately realizing that his tone might be interrogatory. Unsurprisingly, Terrell did not perceive it as such. He didn't take offense to anything, especially anything Darien said.

"Yeah, I'm a little shaken up here." He pointed to his head. "Maybe that's why." Darien let out a slight chuckle. Before he could say anything, the two were shaken to their core by thunder.

"About time," Darien said. "We should go inside."

***

25

The next day, Darien made his way to the University, his footsteps were steady as he quickly walked past the people who had occupied themselves in the meaningless chores of life. A blue mask and a cap on his head concealed his identity. He reached the large metal gate of the university and stopped before entering. As he approached the building, he felt his footsteps getting heavier. Darien tried to ignore his thoughts and kept walking at a steady pace. The pathway he walked was surrounded by large patches of lush green grass on both sides. In front of him was a building constructed when the British were in control. The carving on the stone and the mere architecture of the structure always had him in awe, but not today. Today, he was there to fit a piece in the puzzle of solving his father's murder.

He entered the building and stopped outside a door. A heavy feeling took over his body. His anxiety had been uncontrollable since he had met Lina the other night. He knocked on the door before his thoughts could send him into a spiral.

"Enter," a husky voice called from inside.

Darien held the door knob still for a second before turning it. He pushed the heavy door and entered. Before him was a large oak table with a peculiar design carved on it. It was probably the biggest table he had seen. The large glass window behind the table allowed the sunlight to creep in and illuminate the entire office. A frame on the adjacent wall showed many students sitting in several rows.

Behind the desk, a man in his 60s sat with a cigarette. He was clad in a white dress shirt and light grey suspenders, and his round glasses and gelled-back hair made him seem like a man who meant business. Before Darien could speak, the man stood up and greeted him loudly.

"Darien!" He almost shouted. Even at this age, he seemed ripped. It was evident that he worked out. The man opened his arms and embraced Darien.

"Professor Edwin." Darien smiled as he removed his mask.

Professor Edwin Fort was an old friend of Thomas. In fact, he was one of the few friends of his father that Darien had known since he was a child. The Professor had been a long-time trusted policy advisor to several Presidents throughout history. He was also a cabinet member in President Stuart Anderson's team, the administration that ruled the country before Darien's father.

Darien remembered how Professor Edwin was the first to visit their house after Thomas was murdered. For as long as he could remember, the Professor had been with their family in every difficult time.

"Please," he pointed to the chair across from his. Darien sat down, still nervous about the conversation that was to follow. "So, how have you been? It's been a while," the Professor said as he lightly flicked his cigarette into a leaf-shaped crystal ashtray.

"Not well. That's why I'm sitting here."

"I'm listening." The Professor's face turned serious.

"My father's death. It um-" Darien paused.

"It's been so many years, Darien." Edwin interrupted.

"Exactly. How has everyone been so unfazed about it, Professor?" Darien's tone got aggressive. "The Russians assassinated a serving President of the United States. And no one cared to know why? I can't even believe I'm saying these words. It sounds like something straight out of a fiction novel."

The Professor took another puff as he listened to Darien speak.

"And then my brother got kidnapped and murdered. These are American Presidents we're talking about. What is happening?"

"What do you want from me?"

Darien let out a sigh.

"If anyone knows anything about it, it's you. Help me out, please." Darien almost pleaded.

"What do you know?" Professor Edwin asked in a low voice.

"The two books," Darien said coldly, his eyes slightly narrowing as if he was trying to get something out of the Professor. As soon as Professor Edwin heard these words, his face turned pale. Darien immediately knew he had played his cards right. The Professor put off his cigarette in the ashtray and stood up before locking the door. He slowly walked back to his chair and took off his glasses.

"What do you know about the Two Books? And who told you about it?"

"I'd prefer you answer my questions instead of the other way around, Professor."

Professor Edwin went silent for a minute. He just stared at the floor as Darien felt even more anxious.

"Professor?"

"Yes, I just, I need a minute." He looked visibly shaken.

"Take all the time you need," Darien leaned back on his chair. His anxiousness seemed to go away all of a sudden. He felt like he was in control now.

"I don't know how to say this, Darien."

"Give it to me straight, Professor."

"Back when I was in the CIA, I was stationed inside the Soviet Union. My job was to collect intel and report to Washington. Nothing else." He paused again.

"And?"

"And I did that only for a couple of years until I stumbled upon a rogue Russian group that wanted to overthrow the communist regime in Moscow."

Darien sat upright. He was intrigued at how this was relevant to his father's murder.

"Of course, our objectives were aligned. I mean, the US never thought of dismantling the Soviet Union in such a direct manner, but we did want to destroy communism. The faction called itself

'True Russia.' Their leader, Yevgeny Dobrynin, and I got close. Very close."

Darrien was now fully indulged in the Professor's story. For a brief moment, he forgot why he was there.

"When the Berlin wall came down in Reagan's time, True Russia disintegrated, and there was a power struggle. Yevgeny was brutally tortured before I found him inside an abandoned warehouse somewhere in Siberia. He was bleeding from every opening of his body. His teeth had been pulled out, and he had a hole in his left eye socket." The Professor's face showed pain.

"He told me to go to a location before he bled to death in my arms. I went there. It was an underground tunnel, and it seemed abandoned. I searched it for hours when I found something."

"What?"

Professor Edwin let out a long sigh.

"Professor? I need to know."

"I can't tell you. You should leave."

"I'm not leaving until you give me something."

The Professor got up and left without saying anything else. Darien ran his hands through his hair as the Professor exited the room. His anxiety had returned. He wished he hadn't come here. Darien took out his phone and called Terrell.

"I'm at the university," Darien said.

"To meet the professor?"

"Yes."

"Why didn't you take me?"

"He wouldn't have said anything if you were there."

"What'd he say?"

"He was about to tell me something, and then he stopped. Set up a meet with Lina. I'll tell you the details there."

Darien got up and left the room disappointed. Dark grey clouds had reappeared, and it seemed like it would pour any second.

29

Darrien put on his mask and hurried to his car, which was parked at a distance. He got inside and yelled, hitting the steering wheel with both hands.

***

Terrell, Darien and Lina met at the same place they had met a few nights before. The heavy rain made driving almost impossible, but Terrell somehow managed to. He had already briefed Lina on Professor Edwin. Terrell and Darien reached the rendezvous point at the same time. They acknowledged each other's presence and hurried inside.

Lina looked up at them and got back to her laptop. The two sat down on each side of Lina.

"What have you got?" Darien asked impatiently.

"I'm good, and you?" Lina replied sarcastically.

"I'm sorry, I'm a little shaken right now."

Lina slightly turned the laptop toward them.

"Your Professor Edwin was in possession of the Book of Truth," Lina said plainly.

"What?" Terrell shouted. Darien remained silent. It was too overwhelming for him. He tried to compute what Lina had just said.

"When?" He asked in a low voice, his hand covering his mouth.

"What?" Lina asked.

"When? When did he have it?"

"When he was the Secretary of Homeland Security, back in the Anderson administration."

"What happened then?"

"No idea. But he doesn't have it now. At least, that is what he claims."

Darien got up and left.

Terrell and Darien entered Professor Edwin's office and sat down. The Professor was conducting a class. They waited for about an hour before he walked in. The Professor was startled to see the two boys in his office.

"Good morning." He greeted them pleasantly.

"You had the Book of Truth with you," Darien said, ignoring his greeting.

The Professor stopped in his steps. He looked at Terrell and then continued to walk to his seat.

"And this young man is?"

"None of your concern. Tell me what I need to know."

Terrell could not conceal his surprise. He had never seen Darien speak like this. He remained quiet.

"Yes. I had it," Professor Edwin said after a long pause, his neck slightly elevated. "And I know where it is."

"Tell me," Darien demanded.

"No. It's dangerous for you. I will not put you in that position."

"You don't get to decide that, Professor."

"You'll practically be signing your death warrant. They won't leave you alone."

"Who's they?"

"I think I've answered enough of your questions, Darrien." The Professor got up to leave. As he reached the exit, he was stopped by another one of Darien's questions.

"Do you know who killed my father, Professor Edwin?" Darien asked, still facing the Professor's empty chair.

"You should go," Professor Edwin said before exiting.

Darien had gotten his answer. Terrell looked at him as he stared into the abyss.

Chapter 4
The Demand For A New Leader

Fourteen months before Thomas's death

Micheal met Avienda at one of the president's parties and was struck by her beauty. As soon as the interacted, Michael complimented her, and gave her the attention she needed. She told Michael how Thomas didn't have time and was too busy with negotiations and so, Micheal fulfilled every need of hers. She kept giving him information in exchange foro keeping her satisfied. Michael knew the whereabouts of the book of ideology. As he stepped out of the bathroom, he saw Avienda laying on the bed. She was unclothed beneath the beige silk sheets that covered her upper body. He walked toward the bed before kissing her on the lips.

"Why are you up so early?" She asked in her sleepy voice, her eyes still closed.

"I'm meeting the Chinese Premier today. Don't you remember?"

"Can you stay a little longer?" Avienda asked.

"Not today, love." Michael made a sad face.

"You sound just like Thomas," Avienda said as she tossed herself around.

***

The Chief of Staff walked into the Oval Office where Quintin was reviewing some documents. The curtains on the window behind the desk were drawn but both men could hear the muffled chants of protestors outside the White House.

"Mr. Vice President, we need a quick strategy to suppress these protests. Your approval rating is at an all-time low. We can't win the next election like this."

"I know, Peter. Call Michael. Ask him to meet me here."

"Michael? The Solicitor General?"

"Yes. Let me know when he's here," he replied, implying that Peter should leave.

About thirty minutes later, Michael walked into the office where Quintin embraced him. Quintin was Jonathan's Vice President and after his death, had taken the President's office. They sat down on the sofas as Michael lit a cigarette. He knew why his old friend had called upon him but waited for Vice President Quintin to speak.

"What do you think about these protests, Micheal? He asked with a tinge of nervousness in his voice."

The next day, Solicitor General Michael made his way into the crowd that had grown in number since the previous night. The crowd recognized him, clearing his path so that he could go to the front. Quintin smiled as he watched the crowd disperse on his television. He knew Michael would handle it.

Michael walked into the White House once the crowd went away. He had a smile on his face as he entered the Oval Office. Quintin laughed loudly and hugged his friend.

"How did you do it?" He asked with of nervousness in his voice.

"I don't know, it just happened. I just told them that we'll get to the bottom of it."

"They seem to trust you, Micheal, even more than me."

Micheal smiled. It was the first time he had used the Book of Ideology, and he was eager to learn more about it. He quickly excused himself and left.

Micheal came home from the office to some unseasonably hot weather. Flowers in gardens dropping blooms and birds in the trees exhausted and quiet from the heat. As the evening sunshine burnt the pavement, Micheal hurried inside. He immediately turned the AC down to 60 then flipped on the TV and headed to the bathroom to take a shower. As he was about to enter the bathroom, he stop in his tracks when he heard the news.

"Former President Jonathan's body was found stuffed in sewer manhole in New York City this morning," the reporter said.

***

The next day, Micheal visited late President Thomas's family to pay his respect to Avienda and Darien.

"I was your dad's attorney," Michael introduced himself to Darien. "I am truly sorry for your loss. If there's anything I can do, please let me know." Micheal got up to leave and Darien walked him out to his car.

"How did my father die?" Darein suddenly asked.

Micheal stopped, with the car keys in hand, poised to open the car door.

"I don't know. Why do you ask?"

"You worked for him so I thought you'd know something."

"What do you mean?" Michael became apprehensive.

"Oh, nothing." Darein smiled. "Have a good day. Thank you for coming."

Micheal got into his car and saw Avienda watching from front window.

I need to find out what happened this was not the plan she probably hates me now. Michael thought to himself.

34

The next morning, he got a call from the White House informing him that Quintin wanted to see him. Slightly annoyed, he got ready and headed to meet the Vice President.

"Michael, please sit." Quintin greeted him warmly. "Please get some coffee and donuts," the Vice President said to one of his staff members. "So, Micheal, I'll get straight to the point. I've been thinking about it since yesterday. You see, you're popular, and the people like you. I don't know if I should be saying this, but I think you should run for President in the upcoming elections."

"Will you not be running for office?" Michael asked as he almost spilled his coffee.

"No. I'm already tired. The presidency is too much responsibility and stress. I could maybe become your running mate, what do you say?"

"But I barely passed the bar exam. I don't know how its going to work out," Micheal said, settling himself.

"I'm not asking you to make a decision right away. Take your time, think about it, and then let me know." Quintin smiled.

"Is that all you wanted? Because I have more important stuff to do." Michael stood up.

"Micheal, I saw what you did with the protestors. Don't sell yourself short."

Before Michael could respond, they heard two Congressmen arguing loudly in the corridors right outside the Oval Office about the budget cuts. Quintin stood up and went to the men to calm them down. Instead of lowering their voices, they got even louder. Quintin turned around and walked back to his office. As soon as he walked in, his phone rang and he got busy. Seeing Quintin occupied, Michael quickly walked out.

"Gentlemen, it's not appropriate to argue in the middle of the White House. I'd really appreciate it if you could take your fight someplace else," Michael said.

35

The men, who had ignored the Vice President of the United States, just a few moments ago looked at Michael for a brief moment.

"Sure," one of them said calmly before leaving.

Nine months later - Election Day

It was a cold morning when Attorney Michael woke up in his bed. He looked out the window that overlooked the garden in his Glover Park house. Before he could leave bed, his phone rang. It was his campaign manager, Cameron.

"What's up, Cam?" He asked.

"It's official. We've done it. Congratulations, Mr. President elect!"

Michael smiled. He was excited but he was someone who did not showcase his emotions.

"Congratulations to you too, Cam," he said before disconnecting the call. Letting out a sigh, he turned to find the other side of the bed empty. "Marie!" He yelled.

"Oh, you're up." His fiancé came running inside the room. "Do you have anything? Because the news doesn't. I have been up all night. My anxiety didn't let me sleep." She spoke quickly. It was apparent that she was more concerned about the result than Michael himself.

"Honey, relax." He smiled and stretched out his hand. Marie grabbed it as her fiancé made her sit beside himself on the bed. "Are you relaxed?" He asked.

"Not really."

"Will you be relaxed if I tell you that you're speaking to the President elect of the United States of America?"

Marie let out a loud shriek.

"Are you serious?" She screamed.

"Just got off the phone with Cam. Should be on the news any minute. We managed to win Arizona, Michigan and Florida at the end." Michael smiled.

***

As micheal drove up to the white house, the crowd erupted into cheers. The people loved Michael and the idea of him being President seemed brilliant.

"You all remember your beloved President Thomas. He was executed by the Russians on national television. What did we do? Nothing! I assure you, I will seek revenge from the Russians. Listen hard, Khrushchev! You will not get away with this. Doesn't matter if it's been two decades. We will make you pay. We will restore America's glory!"

The crowd erupted into cheer once again as Quintin continued watching his friend and made him nervous with every word he uttered. He began to realize his political career was practically over. He would never be able to challenge Michael.

Two weeks later

Michael's Chief of Staff ran into the Oval Office where President Michael was sitting with Democrat Senators. They all looked at him, his face showing apparent sign of worry.

"Yes, Shaun?" The President asked.

"Mr. President, may I speak to you in person?"

"No, you may not. I'm busy right now." Michael turned his attention to the Senators again.

"It's –uh. It's important," Shaun said.

"Excuse me," Michael said as he stood up. The two men left the office. "What is it?" Michael asked angrily. Shaun showed him his phone.

37

Michael's face turned pale as he saw what was on the screen. He could hear his own palpitations as he felt a drowning feeling inside of him.

"Where did you get this from?" He asked Shaun after staring at the phone for a few seconds.

"I don't know the source but a reporter from CNN sent me this. And they're going on air with this in a few minutes."

Michael ran his fingers through his hair, not knowing what to do. Shaun just stood by his side. They knew there was nothing they could do to prevent it. Michael stayed silent for a few seconds and then walked inside.

"Gentlemen," Michael said as he reentered the office, "I think we'll have to cut this meeting short." Somehow, he managed to smile.

"Is everything okay, Mr. President?" One of them asked.

"Absolutely. There's an urgent matter I need to attend to."

The Senators left and Michael threw himself on the chair in desperation. He thought about how he would get impeached not before his fiancé would leave him. As he got lost deep in thought, his phone rang. It was Marie.

"*Is it real?*" The text read.

Michael dropped phone back on the table and leaned back on his chair. A video of him and Avienda had gotten out. It was the biggest scandal in the history of the United States: a serving President sleeping with the wife of a former President.

Soon after, Michael's phone began ringing constantly. The scandal was all over the news in a few minutes. Just the next day, protests erupted calling for the President to be impeached. President Michael had lost all the popularity and respect of his nation.

Chapter 5
The War Of Two Nations

6 Weeks Later

"Did they attack?" The Secretary of Defense asked the General.

"Invading our airspace is an attack, Mr. Secretary."

"Go to DEFCON 4, General," the president said.

"I don't think that's necessary, Mr. President."

"Do as I say, General!" President Michael Interrupted.

"Yes, sir! Should we summon the Russian or the Iraqi ambassador, Mr. President?" the secretary of defense asked.

"Not yet." Everyone was surprised at what the president had just said under the given circumstances. The standard operating procedure was to call the diplomatic staff of the hostile Country and sort it out with him, but these were not normal circumstances.

The president had lost his spark as a leader after his affair had become public and his fiancé, Marie, had left him. His ability to make his decisions was already affected. Secretly, Vice President Quinton sees Michael going weak and smiles. He decided to go for the president's spot so that the Russian president would not blackmail him anymore about his secret dealings. Quintin thought to himself, "Tomorrow, I will spread this news to reporters and finish the impeachment of Michael while he's weak.

Michael gets a call in the middle of the night from the chief of staff.

"Iraq attacked Israel! We need you in the situation room right away." Jumping up, Michael thought, this is a chance to redeem myself and prove that he was the one America needed.

He grabbed the book, glanced through it, and rushed to get dressed. Right away, he told the Secret Service driver to step on it. When he arrived at the control room, Antonio was already there

39

with his military commanders. The Director of the CIA and the Secretary of defense were also there. There was tension in the air.

As soon as he sees Michael, he starts briefing him on the situation.

"The Iraqis have Israeli hostages." After hearing this, he smiles inwardly. He tells Antonio to call the ambassador of Iraq and make it clear to him that if the hostages are not returned in five hours, the entire Iraqi palace will be wiped off the planet. Antonio was reluctant to obey his orders, "I do not think that is a good idea, sir..."

Michael stopped him before he finished speaking with a cold stare. "Am I not your commanding chief?"

"Yes, sir."

"Then do it. And I want this story on the front page of every newspaper tomorrow morning. Do it now!" Michael's tone was stern as he left the room while staring at Quintin. Lieutenant Antonio saw Michael's and Quintin's hostile stare.

Now, there was uneasiness in the room. The next day, when the Iraqi president saw the news on the front page, he ordered to release of the hostages, fearing that Michael, the new president, would do what he promised. Later that day, reports of Israel's hostages are released as the Iraqi president publicly apologizes for the rash action of unknown terrorists.

The newspaper tactic worked, and Michael gained overwhelming support from the American people for showing strong leadership. Michael smiled to himself as he sat in front of the TV, satisfied with his decision.

The next morning, Lieutenant Antonio went to Quintin's office and waited for him to return. Quintin greeted the Lieutenant with a smile.

"What can I do for you, Lieutenant?" He asked.

"I know you've been asking questions," Antonio said, ignoring the Vice President's greeting.

"What are you talking about?" Quintin was taken aback.

"I noticed you talking with President Michael's chief of staff."

"It doesn't concern you, Lieutenant. Anything else?" Antonio got up and walked toward the door. He turned around before exiting, stared at Quintin, smiled then exited, closing the door behind him.

Quintin quickly picked up his phone with an encrypted line and dialed a number. A few seconds later, someone answered the phone. "I think we have a problem," he said.

Meanwhile, Antonio sat inside his car, listening through the bug he had planted in Quintin's office. "If you manage to get enough support for us from the public, we might not need to launch an attack." The voice on the other end said.

"I'll speak to you when and if I have something." Quintin disconnected the call.

Three weeks later

Two large groups of people were gathered outside the Capitol, chanting slogans against each other. The Russians and Iraqis had simultaneously attacked the military bases in the Middle East.

Quintin persuaded the President to make him his chief military advisor to strengthen his position with Michael. Because of all that was happening, the public had become divided. By controlling the media, Vice President Quintin's now military advisor had covertly convinced a large number of Russian and Iraqi-American citizens to support the actions of the Russians and Iraqis, who had now attacked their sovereignty twice. The people unaware of the internal political strife inside the White House had bought the narrative Quintin had sold them.

He sat in his office thinking about the future, imagining himself in the Oval Office, making all the decisions from behind the President's desk. To achieve this goal, he was willing to sacrifice many lives. Suddenly, his phone rang, disrupting his thought

41

process. It was the same encrypted phone that he was using to stay in contact with America's enemies. He stared at the phone vibrating at the table. With every ring, he contemplated whether to answer. His position of power made him hesitant, but he knew he had no choice.

"Yes?" He picked up the phone.

"Well done," the voice said. Quintin stayed silent.

One week later.

"I heard you're still asking questions about Michael. What are you looking for? Lieutenant Antonio asked as he walked into the office. Quintin quickly put the phone down and seemed slightly intimidated.

"I don't know what you're talking about, and like I said before, who I talk to is none of your concern.

"It's on my watch Antonio said, smiling as he walked out.

"Next time, make sure you knock before you come in. Antonio paused, "I don't take orders from anyone except the President." Antonio left.

***

Lina Bennett, while doing research on the books ran across another colleague, Kathie Nail. She remembered Kathie as a reporter from Washington, D.C. Kathie was an intelligent and fearless journalist when unearthing impossible secrets. Searching her reporter phone list, she found Kathie's number and gave her a call to see if she was willing to help unlock the location of the two books. As she was on call, Lina received a call from Terrell. When she was done with Kathie, she called Terrell back.

"She asked you called?

"Did you watch the news?" Terrell asked.

"Yeah, I did. So what do you think? He seems like an intelligent, stern, no-nonsense President," Lina replied.

"No. It doesn't make sense."

"What do you mean?"

"Have you ever seen a government backtrack just because the President said so? It doesn't work like that. Something's up."

"Maybe. Anyway, I found another reporter to help us with this mystery we're in," Lina told him.

"Another reporter? Who?"

"Kathie Nails. She's Washington-based."

"Kathie Nails sounds familiar. Can she be trusted?" Terrell asked.

"um, that name sounds familiar. I knew a Kathie when I was growing up."

"Let's meet her."

Terrell immediately called Darien to let him know about Lina's newfound resources.

"Can I call you back?" Darien said as his mother walked into the room. He knew he couldn't let his mother know about any of this.

"Ah, better yet, set up a meeting with Lina. I can meet you there. "

"Okay."

***

Terrell got off the phone with Darien and got into his navy blue Mustang. As he maneuvered his way through the thick traffic,

he didn't want to eat a microwave dinner.

He thought about going to the cafe for dinner but quickly changed his mind. The sky above him was dark grey, and it was apparent that it was about to rain.

As he turned around to go home, Terrell decided to call Lina.

"Hey, when would it be a good time to meet?" Terrell asked. "To talk about Michael and the books."

"We can meet this weekend," Lina said. "Kathie is on her way. She'll be here too by then."

As he finished the call, Terrell looked up and saw the signal light turn yellow. He quickly floored the mustang pedal and managed to cross it just as the light turned red. Terrell smiled to himself.

"Still got it!" He exclaimed, turning in Rainbow Estate Street. Terrell lived in a posh area with a retired military carnal. He pulled into a two-storied complex-style plantation house with a round driveway and drove in, parking next to his ninja bike call sign. guilt

He texted Darien about the meeting that had been set for Saturday night.

"1800 same cafe. Sounds good?"

"Yes. Darien replied."

"Also, she's bringing a reporter friend from D.C."

"Wait! What? Who!"

"Don't worry. Lina trusts her."

Lina headed to the cafe to do a little research on Michael. While driving, she called Kathie to make sure she was coming down.

"Hey, there," Lina said. "Let's meet at the cafe on Moreland Avenue, where we met the last time?"

"The café with sunflowers out front and that AC with the ticking sound?" Kathie confirmed.

"That's the one!"

"Alright, perfect! See you on Saturday."

As Lina entered the café, she spotted a blonde-haired, blue-eyed, tall good-looking guy.

"Huh! Never seen him here before. He must be new. Probably military."

44

Quintin looked over at her, but she didn't notice him looking. "She's probably a reporter.". He thought to himself.

***

As Darien went to work on Saturday morning, Terrell reminded him of the meeting.

"Let me just finish up here. I'm going home for a quick shower, then head over."

"Be there at 18:00, or you're buying dinner for all of us."

Darien laughed to himself.

Just before 18:00, Terrell's car pulled up to the entrance of the café, followed by Darien's. He stepped out of the car and smiled at Terrell.

"Look like you're buying your own dinner tonight."

Terrell laughed. As they entered the café, Lina and Kathie were already sitting there having coffee. Lina immediately waved at Darien and Terrell. Darien glimpsed at his watch and went inside.

"Hi, Guys. This is Kathie. Kathie, Terrell, Darien. We all are up to speed about the whole situation."

"Do I know you?" Terrell asked Kathie as he sat down, not sure that was the same girl he went to school with

"I think you do. What school did you go to?" Kathie asked Terrell.

"Booker T. Washington."

"You've got to be kidding me! Are you the same Terrell who slammed the car doors?"

Darien almost spilled his coffee as he laughed loudly.

Terrell smiles with a sheepish smile.

"That's me!" Terrell admitted. He had recognized Kathie. "How have you been? Looks like you grew up to become a hot-shot journalist, eh?"

"You're overselling me. I just happen to work at the White House. I cover small parties."

Terrell and Kathie talked for a while before Lina interrupted.

"Can we talk about the case first? You guys can catch up later."

"Sure," Kathie said.

"This is what I have on Michael. Grew up in Riverdale, Georgia, and went to college here. Looks like he barely passed the bar exam before moving to D.C. He worked as an attorney for your father for seven years. That's all I got." Lina stopped talking. "What do you know about him?" she looked at Kathie.

"All I know about him is that he's super smart and a very hard-working man. But he's also an opportunist."

"What about you guys? Did you find anything new?" Lina asked Darien and Terrell.

"My friend knows about the book, but he won't tell me where it is. He thinks it is too dangerous. I met Michael once. He came over to give his condolences to my family after my brother's death. I asked him how my father died, and he had this funny look on his face, saying he didn't know. I think he knows more than he was telling," Darien replied.

At that moment, a guy sitting three tables from them overheard them speaking about the books. He stopped eating and went still.

"Khrushchev will be glad to hear this," Quintin said to himself. Kathie is the most intuitive of them all. "I think we should discuss this later," she said, looking over Darien's shoulder and seeing the guy sitting very still.

"I agree," Terrell said. They all finished eating and then left. About half an hour later, Quintin left the cafe.

***

Antonio, having nothing to do replayed the conversation he had just heard, thinking about what happened to the first President. Suddenly, he got up and rushed back to Quintin's office. However,

just as he pulled up to park, he saw Quintin showing up. Without wasting any time, Antonio quickly turned on the bug in his car.

Inside his office, Quintin dialed the encrypted number, and someone answered the call.

"I have the name of the subject with knowledge of the books. Kathie Nail and three other unknowns. I will let you know when I have the location." The line disconnected without an answer.

Antonio was stunned as much as he was confused. It did not make sense to him. What books? He thought to himself.

Quintin sat down, turned on his computer and began his research about Kathie Nail. He found out that she grew up in New York and graduated from Stanford University with a bachelor's degree in political science. Kathie moved to D.C., got a scholarship in journalism, and was well known for unearthing impossible stories. Quintin smiled.

***

Kathie was staying in the Wyndham Downtown Club in Atlanta. As she sat down, she jotted down something on a piece of paper.

First, I'll wrap Terrell around my finger. Next Lina. She'll be easy. And lastly, Darien, the unknown piece of the puzzle, the hardest lock to pick now! PUT on a break' em down outfit. A little skin, a little innocence and I can be trusted. No need to wait. I'll pick your story to the bone. I am the Best reporter of the year. This story is mine.

Kathie quickly picked up the phone and called Terrell.

"Hello?" Terrell answered.

"Hey, Kathie here."

"Kathie! How are you?" Terrell asked excitedly.

"I'm good, and you?"

"I'm good too."

"Terrell, I was thinking if you were free tomorrow?" There was a tinge of seductiveness in her voice.

"I am. I've got the whole day to myself."

"Oh, perfect. Can I come over then?" She asked.

"Sure. What time?"

"Noon?"

"Noon sounds good. See you then. I'll text you my address."

The next morning, Kathie pulled out an outfit that she knew would surely break Terrell. She got ready and observed herself in the mirror. Quickly, she got into her Mercedes and called Terrell.

"I'm on my way. I know this is earlier than we decided on, but I couldn't wait." As she drove, she saw a black SUV following her. She ignored it and turned into Terrell's street while the SUV continued to go straight. Terrell's house seemed nice. Before she could think anything else, she saw Terrell come out.

As soon as he spotted Kathie, he smiled. She looked beautiful, and her attire was quite suggestive.

Wow! Not being married really does have its benefits. He thought to himself. Kathie got out of the car and hugged Terrell before they went inside.

"Have a seat, please. Tea? Coffee? You name it?" Terrell asked.

"Tea would do, thanks!"

A few minutes later, Terrell brought in tea for her.

"To be honest. I wasn't too interested in this case, I'm still not. But when I knew you were involved, I changed my mind." She smiled. "Okay, you tell me everything you know."

48

"That's gonna take a while," Terrell said. "But here we go," Terrell spoke for three hours, going through every detail of the case. When he was done, Kathie just stared at him, smiling. Her scent, smile and eyes told Terrell to make a move.

"What am I doing?" Terrell thought to himself. Before he could look away, Kathie gently grabbed his face and kissed him.

"Stay here," Terrell immediately suggested. "I have lots of rooms here. No need to waste your money on the hotel."

"I will, on one condition. You show me your house. I love it, and I'd like to see the rest of it."

"Deal!"

***

Quintin picked up the phone and sent an encrypted message.

"Need cleaning supplies. I have a little stain."

"How much?"

"Three, it's a tough one."

"On the way."

"Now that's that done, let's find my lucky charm," he said to himself." He called Homeland Security and asked about the whereabouts of Kathie Nail. In less than five minutes, Quintin had the address of where she was staying.

Chapter 6

Revelation Of Betrayal

The President of Ukraine asked for Michael's help to fight Russia. Michael sent military artillery aid, but Ukraine took advantage of Michael's goodwill by stealing the aid money and selling the weapon to terrorists for millions for self-gain.

Antonio, monitoring military weapons and seeing the aid misuse, spoke to Michael. Quintin overhears this and tries to fix the computer report, hoping that this may tarnish Michael and make him look bad. This continued for 8 months until Ukraine asked for more aid. But this time, Lieutenant Antonio gets proof of the aid misuse. He had decided to search the evidence reports from known terrorist groups. On getting a physical video, Antonio shows the President. Michael believes what he sees and decides to confront the Ukrainian President about this betrayal.

The Ukraine president doesn't take this news well and fires cabinet members who were known for corruption and bribes. But this move has little impact on Michael, who already feels betrayed; he knows if this gets out, America will be a laughingstock around the world.

This needs to stop before America's reputation is ruined, thinking to himself, "Enough is enough!" and leaves the Office Early.

He goes home to read certain sections from the book Of Ideology as he can't sleep. Later that night, the president calls the lieutenant. Antonio was up eating a midnight snack when the special encrypted phone rang. He knew that it was the president. He answers.

"Yes, sir. Mr. President."

"I have a mission for you."

"Yes, sir. What can I do?"

"The problem between Russians and Ukraine must stop now. Go to Alaska and wipe the Russian mine facility out. And do not leave any evidence. I need this done by morning."

"Sir, by morning? Impossible."

"Are you an American Navy seal? Speak up."

"Yes, sir."

"The word impossible is not in navy seal vocabulary."

"No, sir."

"I don't want to ever hear that word from my special ops lieutenant again."

"Yes, sir."

"No ifs and buts about it. Listen carefully, Lieutenant. Wipe the Russian facility off the face of this planet. It's an order. Do it now."

"And don't call me sir. I will tell Quintin in the morning to announce a withdrawal of US Aid for Ukraine and that the US is taking over Diomedes Island off the coast of Alaska. There will be no more drilling in Alaska, and if anyone attacks the US sovereignty land, retaliation will be swift and severe." After Antonio hears the president's plans, he grabs the phone tighter and smiles, saying to himself, "This is my chance to redeem the American military's honor."

Lieutenant Antonio, Calls the top special ops team. Laying out the president's plan. "You have 5 hours. Take 15 of the SR72 "Darkstar" fighter jets to the Russian drilling facility in Alaska and level it, leaving nothing standing. Gentlemen, American military's reputation depends on this mission. And my job. If you don't succeed, don't bother coming back. Antonio looked each man in the eyes sternly no one blinked. Let's get it done," the lieutenant concluded.

Within 3.5 hours, 15 stealth SR72 "Darkstar" fighter jets flew at Mark 2, hitting their targets and returned at 0400

Lieutenant Antonio gets the call

"It's done!"

He calls the president. Michael picks' up and hears one word "done."

He hangs up

The next morning, Michael calls Quintin to his office.

"Mr. President. You asked for me?"

"I need you to make this announcement to the nation. He handed Quintin an envelope.

"It's all written out here."

"Yes, sir." With that, Quintin left Michael's office.

***

Edwin sat in his classroom office, contemplating the events about former president Thomas, Jonathan and the things unfolding in the world and the significance of the Book of Truth. He realized that if anything were to happen to him, the knowledge and power within the Book of Truth would be lost. So he resolved to trust Darien with the book's location and how to use it before anything untoward happens to him.

Calling Darien late on Monday night, the phone rang, and Darien picked up.

"Hello."

"It's your mentor, Professor Edwin. Darien, I need you to come down right away. It's about the book. I want to tell you about it."

"You alone, no one else. If you bring anyone, I won't tell you."

Darien, understanding the urgency, promptly made his way to Edwin's office, alone as instructed. Upon arrival, Darien was greeted by Edwin,

"How are you doing, son?"

"I'm okay. Um, coming here at midnight was a little unexpected. But I understand it's important."

Edwin glimpsed outside, ensuring they were undisturbed, and began to disclose the vital knowledge about the book.

"Darien, what I'm about to share with you is of utmost importance. It may alter the course of your life and potentially place you in peril," Edwin said, fixing his gaze on Darien.

This is as serious as it gets.

Edwin proceeded to detail the significance of the Book of Truth, its contents, and its responsibility.

"This book holds the key to understanding the book of ideologies that have shaped our world. It contains invaluable insights into its previous guardians, their actions, and its current whereabouts," he explained earnestly. "You must promise to safeguard this knowledge, disclosing it to one only as necessary, yet never relinquishing its possession to anyone."

Darien nodded solemnly, acknowledging the weight of the responsibility bestowed upon him. Edwin then divulged the book's location, situated in Edwin's hometown of Ocala, Florida, within a library on Main Street adjacent to the bowling alley. He provided specific instructions for retrieving the book and emphasized the importance of keeping it secure, warning of the potential risks associated with its possession.

"As for how to use the book," Edwin continued, his tone grave yet resolute, "when you open it, there will be no pages, just white inside cover. Turn the book over. Concentrate on the back cover, and the words revealing its history and current status will materialize."

Edwin continues, "Darien don't forget what this book stands for. Keep it safe and uphold integrity."

"This isn't about power," Edwin insisted. "It's about preserving knowledge and truth, ensuring a better future for our nation. Remember, protect the book, and it will guide you towards a brighter tomorrow."

***

As Darien left Edwin's office and got into his car, he contemplated the urgency of his mission. "If I leave now," he thought, "I can reach the Ocala library by 8:00 in the morning." Along the way, he remembered his friend Terrell and decided to give him a call.

"Hey, who's calling this early?" Terrell groggily answered.

"It's Darien. Listen, I just left Edwin's office, and he finally told me where to find the book."

"Ah, so he finally came around?"

"Yes, I'll be out of town for just one day."

"Why didn't you swing by and pick me up?"

"Edwin made me promise to come alone, or he wouldn't have told me. Keep an eye on Mom until I get back. Once I have the book and I'm on my way home, I'll call you."

"Alright, be careful."

"Yeah, no problem."

Darien drove through the night, stopping only around 5:00 AM for a cup of coffee to stay awake. By 7:55 AM, he arrived at the Ocala library and waited in the parking lot. When the receptionist arrived, Darien followed her inside.

"May I help you?" she asked.

"Give me 539," Darien requested.

She squinted at him, silent.

Darien tried again. "Give me 539 from Edwin Coley."

She smiled, reached into her desk, and handed him a set of keys. "Go three halls to your right, turn left at the end of the hall, and the last door on the right. Use the key to go inside. There are three safety deposit boxes on the wall. Find the one marked 539, use the combination key to open it, and what you're looking for is inside."

"Thank you," Darien replied, taking the keys.

Following her directions, Darien found the box, opened it, and retrieved the thin book. He hesitated to open it but decided against it and left quickly, returning the keys as he exited the library. Placing the book in the glove box of his car, he smiled with excitement as he drove off.

Halfway back, he remembered to call Terrell. "I got it," he informed him.

"O man good. I should be back in town in three hours."

"Alright, see you then."

Arriving back at noon, Darien called Terrell. "Where are you?"

"At lunch. Meet me back at my place in 20 minutes."

"Okay, on my way."

When Terrell arrived, Darien briefed him on Edwin's strict instructions. "We either do this right, or it won't work," he emphasized. "I'll examine the book's secrets and tell you what it reveals. Keep this between us."

"Got it," Terrell nodded.

Darien explained the book's supposed functions and decided to call Terrell once he finished examining it. As Terrell left, Darien went to his downstairs den, retrieved the book from its hidden compartment, and sat down to concentrate on Edwin's instructions.

Opening the book, Darien found it blank inside. Turning to the back cover and concentrating, words gradually appeared, revealing shocking information about past holders of the book. As the words disappeared, Darien trembled, securing the book and heading upstairs to call Terrell.

"Where are you?" Terrell answered.

"I just got home. I've already found out what we needed to know," Darien replied, deciding to meet with Lina and Kathie the next day at the café.

"Alright, call Lina and Kathie, have them meet us at café"

"Sounds good."

***

Terrell made a call to Lina. "Hello, this is Terrell. Darien wants us to meet at the cafe tomorrow night at 6:00 PM. Can you make it?"

Lina agreed, "Yes, okay. I'll be there."

Terrell then phoned Kathie. "Hey, where are you?"

"I'm downtown shopping."

"Okay, can you join us at the cafe at 6:00 PM tomorrow night? Darien has something really important to share."

"Sure, I'll be there," Kathie replied.

With the calls made, Terrell confirmed with Darien that everything was set. "Okay, good. You come early, around 5:00, so we can talk privately and decide how much to tell Kathie and Lina."

"Okay," Darien agreed.

Terrell decided to call off work for the rest of the day, took a shower, got dressed, and glanced at his watch. It was almost 5:00 PM. He opted to ride his motorcycle, Guilt, enjoying the nice weather with clear skies and light traffic. As he approached a traffic light, he thought to himself, "This traffic light doesn't like me for some reason. It will turn red." He hit the throttle, blasting through, just as the light turned red. Grinning as he noticed a cop trying to give chase. He got serious guilt, jumping from 80 to 120 in 9.2

56

seconds. The cop flashing light quickly disappeared in his rearview mirror. After about half a mile, the cop gave up.

Looking up, seeing the café approaching fast, gearing down, Terrell found a good parking spot glimpsed at his watch 7 minutes, not bad. He went inside, remembering Lina's favorite table. He ordered a salad and relaxed, waiting for Darien's arrival.

About ten minutes later, Darien pulled up in his midnight blue BMW, spotting Terrell inside. Darien smiled, parked beside Terrell's bike, and joined him at the table.

"Whose bike is that outside? Nice ride," Darien remarked.

Terrell grinned. "You like it?" Darien, smiling, handed him an envelope. "I wrote down everything so we don't have to talk out loud." Terrell pulls out the letter and begins to read it.

Khrushchev, the Russian president.

Book of Ideology.

Action: Destroy the Soviet Union.

Edwin Coley. Ah, are you kidding me? Took the book of Ideology to American President Thomas.

"No"

Action: Attorney Michael stole the Book of Ideology from President Thomas.

"Can you believe this?"

"Ah not so loud."

"Oh, okay, sorry."

Michael's action saved Israel's hostages from Iraq. He destroyed the Diomede Island resource facility off the coast of Alaska. The Book of Ideology remains with Michael.

"Oh man, Khrushchev didn't get but one chance to use it. Is that why he's so mad? We can thank Professor Edwin."

"Ya, good thing too. Your father had the book but didn't get a chance to use it. Michael stole it. So that's what the email was about. Michael and Thomas having words before his death."

"Ya, I thought Michael knew more than he was telling."

They realized the seriousness of the situation. Lina and Kathie arrived a few minutes later, seeing Darien and Terrell in the café come over sat down. Terrell asked Lina and Kathie if anyone wanted to order. Lina? No, just coffee. Kathie? Vanilla chocolate mocha smiling. Darien? No, I'm good, just water. Okay, now business. Darien suggested they keep their conversation discreet, handing them envelopes with the information.

As Lina and Kathie read through the contents, they expressed shock and curiosity about the source of the information. Terrell urged caution, sensing potential surveillance. Kathie recalled seeing two black SUVs in the parking lot, sparking concern about possible surveillance by the FBI or unmarked cops.

Deciding to reconvene another time, they left the cafe separately. Lina and Kathie first. Then Darien left to make sure they got home safe. Terrell grinned, confident in his motorcycle, and was the last to depart. Darien hey! Be careful, man. I'm good. 10 minutes later, as he rode off, he waved at the SUVs, noting their non-response. He pulled off black SUVs, following him. The SUV driver said to the passenger, "This must be who we're looking for."

The passenger replies, "No, the boss said it's a woman named Kathie Nail. The driver called the boss. The phone was picked up, and only silence was heard. The driver said, "We're following one now. We couldn't follow the target. She was with two others."

"Okay, keep following. he may lead you to target." The phone goes dead.

He looked over and kept following. Terrell was cruising around 65 when the SUV was still trailing. Terrell, smiling, increases speed.

"You want to play?

The driver of the SUV is shocked. "Oh, Man. What he's doing?" Ahead, he sees a traffic light. He gets almost through before

58

it turns red, hitting the throttle and blowing through the signal. The Cop was sitting on the side. The SUV driver slams on the brakes, cursing! He had to stop. He looks over at the cop car and decides to break off.

Terrell made his way home through back roads, ensuring that he was not being followed. Upon arriving home and entering, the phone rang. "Hey, it's Darien. Lina said that Kathie is heading to her place to talk."

"That SUV was following me, but I managed to lose them."

"Oh man, be careful. see you tomorrow, okay?"

Chapter 7

The Temptation Of Power

"Lina, can you call Darien and tell him we'll be okay? I'm going over to your house to discuss things."

"Sure."

"Hey Darien, Kathie is going over to my place to discuss a few things,"

Lina hangs up the phone, turns in the driveway, and parks. They go inside and sit down.

Kathie. I should publish this. I have more sources and lots of connections in DC. That will make it easier and give me more protection."

Against the higher-ups? Okay, if you think that's safe, I will talk with my colleague. We have an underground anonymous website we use if you run into problems. This is serious; you should be careful,"

"Okay, no problem. I'll get my stuff and leave for DC tonight."

The black SUV had put a bug on Kathie's car to track her. Kathie gets up and leaves Lina's place. When she left, they were waiting. She gets in her car and pulls out. On her way, she calls to book a flight back to DC. Then she sees a black SUV following her through the rearview mirror, so she hangs up and calls Terrell right away.

"Hello, Terrell. This is Kathie. I have a black SUV following me. I'm headed back to your place to get my stuff and leave for DC tonight."

As she hangs up with Terrell, another SUV blocks her at the traffic light. She stops, they jump out, grab her, snatch her into the SUV, and then take off.

Terrell thinks to himself, "What's taking so long? It's been 20 minutes." Terrell decides to take his bike and backtrack to Lina's place. He jumps on his bike, approaches the traffic light, and sees a lot of flashing lights. He thinks to himself, "What's going on?" While driving up to the lights, he sees a Mercedes car with the door open and no one inside at the traffic light. He recognizes it. He jumps off his bike, rushing up. "Hey, what's happening?"

He's frantically looking around. Someone abandoned this car at the traffic light. "No, I know this person."

"Who? Kathie Nail?"

"Okay, officer, report identification over the radio. SUV speeding down the back road, Kathie was knocked out in the back of the SUV."

The cleaner calls the encrypted phone. Quintin picks up and remains silent.

The cleaner says, "We have the stain."

"Okay, good. Bring her to DC. We'll make her talk."

"What about the others?"

"They are not important now. We'll get them later."

"Yes, sir."

Terrell, after hearing the cop say possible kidnapping, thinks to himself, "Lina." He jumps on his bike, burning rubber a quarter of a mile, trying to get to Lina's place. When he gets there, he jumps off his bike and runs, hammering on the door, "Hey Lina, Hey Lina!"

She comes to the door and opens it. "Terrell, what's wrong with you?"

"Kathie's been kidnapped"

"What? You're kidding?"

"No, her car was empty, sitting at the traffic light with cops everywhere."

"What? Oh, no. How?"

They went inside and called Darien. "Hello, this is Terrell. You won't believe it. Kathie's been taken."

"What? No, you've got to be kidding me."

"And she has one of the letters."

"Okay, I think we know who took her. You remember the black SUV at the café in the parking lot?"

"Yeah. Oh man, okay, I'll consult the book. We may be able to reach her in time."

"Alright, man, but hurry.

Lina follows Terrell over to Darien's house. When they got there, Darien had already consulted the Book of Truth, and it didn't tell them anything about Kathie. He asked Lina and Terrell.

Darien says, "Okay, so she said she's headed back to DC, right? Maybe she was followed from DC and kidnapped back to DC. So let's find someone to help from DC."

They started discussing if they knew anyone in DC."I know the attorney who worked for my father," Darien says, "I only knew Kathie, and she was kidnapped," Lina adds. Don't ask. I don't know anyone from DC," Terrell says. Darien's mother, coming in from work, overhears them and sticks her head in his room. "Darien, is everything okay?"

"Yes, Mom."

"I heard you talking about the attorney from DC, Michael.

"Yes, Michael. He visited us after Jonathan's death. We were discussing who knew someone in DC. We need to get in touch with someone up there ASAP! The reporter that was down here with us disappeared, and we need someone in DC to help find her. FBI, cops, anyone, to find out where she is."

"I have Michael's number,"

"Okay, great! Oh wait, he's the president now. That won't work," Darien says.

Avienda says, "Trust me, he will answer."

She goes out to call Michael's private number. He sees the caller ID and answers. "Hello, Avienda. It's good to hear from you. How are you?"

"Hi, Michael. I have a favor to ask. My son has a friend, reporter Kathie Nail, from DC, who was down visiting, and she disappeared. Can you look into this for me?"

"Okay, for you, no problem. Right away"

"Thank you."

Michael hangs up and then calls the Chief of Staff. "Shawn, I need to get the Secret Service to call Langley and have them find out where this reporter, Kathie Nail, is."

"Yes, sir."

Then Michael calls Lieutenant Antonio to his office. "I have another small problem you might be able to help with."

"Yes, sir."

"We have a reporter kidnapped. I would like you to look into this. See what you can find out about it."

"Yes, sir."

When Antonio left the office, he saw Quintin going to his office. Antonio decided to go to his car, turn on the bug, and listen in. He heard Quintin say, "Ok, Good. Bring her to DC. We'll make her talk. Let me know when you're here."

The phone picked up silent. Quintin said, "I have someone who can tell me where the book is. I will have the location tomorrow." Then he hung up.

The next evening, Quintin picked up and remained silent. The cleaner said, "We're here." He hung up before Antonio could turn off the bug. He heard the phone dialing again. "Here, we have the stain."

"Okay, good. Put her in a secure spot and let me know where."

"Yes, sir."

One hour later, he got a call. He picked up and remained silent. "We're in a warehouse at 20th Street and Main in Columbia District."

"Okay, I'll be right there." They took Kathie, untied her, and tied her to a chair. She woke up.

"Who are you? Do you know who I am? I'm a Washington DC news reporter."

The cleaner said, "Just be quiet." Kathie looked around, not knowing where she was.

"I have rights!" Kathie says, but the cleaners don't respond.

In 20 minutes, Quintin shows up. When Kathie sees him walk in, she gasps with surprise. "Vice president Quintin. You kidnapped me?"

"Yes, you have something I want. You give me what I need, and you can walk free." Kathie looked around but couldn't figure out where she was.

Quintin said, "Where is the book?" Kathie said, "What book? I don't know what you're talking about."

"Don't play games with me. I was there in Atlanta at the café; I overheard you talking about the book, so don't play dumb with me. Tell me where the book is."

"I don't have it," Kathie said.

"Did you search her?" Quintin asks the Cleaner.

"Yes, she just had this envelope." He handed it to Quintin. Opening it, he smiled, and his grin went wide. "Well, it looks like you have it all written down. Ok, guys, see if she knows anything else. And when you're finished... well, you know."

Quintin walked away with the envelope. He thought to himself, "Wow, who knew Michael had the book of ideology?" Behind him, he could hear Kathie begin to scream. The cleaner got the other three friends out of her, and then they killed her. Quintin went back to his office to make a phone call. But before he could, the phone

64

rang. He picked up and remained silent. The cleaner said, "It's done. What do you want us to do with the body?"

"Let's send a message. Take it to New York City. Stuff it in a sewer manhole."

"Yes, sir."

"We have the names of the other three: Terrell, Darien, and Lina."

"Ok, you guys did good. Take a week off. I'll be in touch."

"Yes, sir."

Quintin hung up and dialed another number. The phone rang two times. Then it was picked up. Silent on the other end. Quintin says, "I have the location of the books, but we have a problem."

"I sent you 4 cleaners. What do you mean we have a problem?"

"The problem is who has the book. The President of the United States has the book."

"I see. Uh, it doesn't matter. You listen to me. I need that book, or else."

"Ok, it may take a while." The phone went dead.

Antonio thinks to himself, "So, Quintin is involved. We need to bring the President up to speed on what Quintin is up to. Call the President."

"Yes, Lieutenant," the president says

"I have something you need to know."

"Already?"

"Yes, sir, but it's more about your Chief Military Advisor."

"Ok, I have a meeting with the Washington press just after noon. Let's discuss this in the morning. 08 00 in my office."

"Thank you, sir." Antonio was there at 0800 sharp. Michael was in his office. "Lieutenant, come in." "What did you find out?" asks the President. "Well, sir, I found out through an unauthorized bug that I placed in Quintin's office. I know it was wrong, but..."

"Lieutenant, this better be good."

"But, sir, hear me out. I found out Quintin is involved with the reporter's kidnapping."

"Keep talking."

"Yes, sir. I have this recording through the bug. I want you to listen to it."

Antonio takes out the recorder and plays it for President Michael. "Okay, good. Bring her to DC. We'll make her talk." Then, the president hears the dialing tone. "I have the location of the book. But there's a problem. The president of the United States has the book. Click. Tap. Stop.

Michael leans back in his chair, thinking to himself. "So, Quintin kidnapped the reporter, Kathie Nail, and knows I have the Book of Ideology. And this other person, the associate he's dealing with... who is he?"

Michael looks at Lieutenant Antonio before saying, "You did well. Keep your bug there. If it's found, tell the Secret Service I authorized it."

"Yes, sir."

"Okay, lieutenant, Carry on and find this reporter."

"Yes, sir."

Antonio got up and said, "Thank you, sir." He then leaves to find Kathie Nail. Michael calls Shawn. "Shawn, get me the records of all calls Quintin made in the last six months."

"Yes, sir."

"Have secret service trace Quintin. I would like to know where he goes, who he talks to, and what he does during his off time."

"Yes, sir."

"Do you have any information on this news reporter?"

"Yes, sir. We received a call from New York City troops. A young woman's body was found in the sewer drain on the main street."

"Ok, has any of this reached the public yet."

66

"No, sir. The FBI is still investigating."

"Ok. Keep it quiet for now."

"Yes, sir."

"You may leave," Michael says, leaning back thanking "Avienda. They will be after her next."

Michael moves forward, grabs his phone, and starts dialing. "Hello, Avienda. This is Michael."

"Yes?"

"Can you and your son come to DC for a while? It looks like some people here in Washington may want you, so you may be in danger."

"I don't think that's a good idea."

"I need you in the witness protection. Don't worry. No one will know you're here. Trust me"

"Okay,"

"I will send Secret Service with a private plane to pick up you, Darien, and his friends involved with Kathie. In the morning? Can you be ready by then?"

"Yes."

"9 AM. Okay?" Michael concludes and hangs up the phone.

After a little while, Shawn walks into the president's room. "Anything on the records?"

"Yes, it looks like he made three calls to Russia, two calls to Atlanta, and received two local calls here in DC, and the last call from the New York City area."

Michael says, "Okay, good."

Michael hangs up and swivels his chair toward the Oval Office window, thinking. It's time to throw out deadwood and clean up this place. It's time to put the Book of Ideology to use again."

The next morning, Michael tries to rattle Quintin into revealing signs of guilt. Michael calls Quintin to his office. "Quintin, come in."

"Yes, Mr. President."

"Have a seat. I would like you to look into this reporter, Kathie Nail. She went missing about two days ago."

Quintin's eyes went wide. He catches himself and regains composure. "Kathie Nail. Sure, okay."

Michael notices Quintin's eyes go wide and his composure changes. "Can you get on that right away?"

Quintin gets up and leaves the office, shaken inside, thinking, "How could he know so quickly?" Michael told the secretary, "I'll be out the rest of the day." "Yes, sir," Michael goes home and consults the book of ideology. Now, he knows exactly what he needs to do.

Two days later, he goes back to the office. "Call the Lieutenant in."

When the Lieutenant arrives, he asks him, "How long have you been with us?"

"Seven years, sir."

"I have a job more dangerous than you've ever pulled before. If you can complete this one, I will promote you to the Head Ghost Ops Commander. Are you up for it?"

"Yes, sir."

"Don't say yes before you hear what I'm asking."

"Okay, sir."

"I need you to devise a plan to kill the Russian president without any evidence leading back to me, but Khrushchev and the world need to know he's going to die without a doubt, giving the Russian nation time to set up his successor."

"Oh, okay."

"Something wrong, Lieutenant?"

"No, no, sir."

"Okay, good man." Antonio leaves the office trembling, excited, and determined. He goes back to his office, sits down, thinks over the president's request, and then collects himself. "If we can pull this one off, America will regain military respect around the world again."

So Antonio called in his special ops team. "Guys, we have a mission more dangerous even than the Alaskan mission."

"Okay, what is it?"

"Michael wants the Russian president killed with no trace leading to him, but wants the world to know before it happens."

"Oh, what? You kidding us? This is a joke, right?"

"No, I just walked out of the president's office with this request. He needs it done in 3 weeks."

"What?"

"Look, do you want America's military to be respected again?"

"Yes, sir."

"Then stop your whining and let's get it done."

Meanwhile, Michael thinks to himself, "We should leave Quintin alive. Let him take the fall for this. Traitor. Yes, he should die in the trap of his own making." Michael smiles.

Lieutenant Antonio, leaving the situation room, grabs his suit jacket, stops by the president's office, and asks permission for 2 days off to plan and strategize.

"Mr. President, I need 2 days to plan and implement the request." Michael, facing the window watching wild birds migrating south, deep in thought, lifts his hand and waves okay to Antonio. "Thank you, sir," leaving the office.

Outside, he could hear the wild geese squawking as they flew south, noticing storm clouds, thinking to himself, "Wish I could go south too. It's about to be a real storm soon." Putting on his jacket, he hops into his electric armored jeep and heads home for some deep-tank thinking. He always thinks better in the cabin he bought in the forest after leaving active field duty. Arriving at the cabin, he sees deer at the foot of the mountain eating grass and a lone gray wolf in the thicket watching the deer. He smiles, thinking to himself, "That's what I would be doing to my enemies." Then, going into the cabin, he deactivates booby traps, clears every room, puts a pot of coffee on the stove, pulls a plant-based chicken out of the freezer for later, sits down at the kitchen table, looking out the kitchen window, thinking, "How to tell a country your president will be assassinated without everyone knowing who it is, and there is nothing you can do? Now, that's a real skill and executing the person without fail, smiling." The coffee pot whistles. He grabs a cup of coffee, sets back down with a notepad, and starts planning.

"Put the fear of God into your enemy."

"Disguise your weapon as something harmless and natural."

He gets on the phone and calls the head NASA engineer. "Yes, this is Lieutenant, Secret Ops Commander."

"Yes, sir."

"Is it possible to have a man-made meteor disguised as a real meteor falling from space, detectable only as a natural rock? This meteor will have three devices inside it. First, an air detractor able to distract all air within a one-foot radius. Second, a device with a two-pronged fork shaped like snake teeth, able to inject coral snake venom. Third, a three-inch-long hypodermic needle electrically charged, able to penetrate the brain and neutralize vision. All three devices must be able to fly, something like the Mars helicopter, with a traveling range of 50 miles, but smaller like an insect, with microscopic cameras and camouflage for hiding."

The NASA engineer asked, "Who will be financing the project?" "Washington. The contact code is deniability. All requests are to go through the Lieutenant Commander. Make this project top priority. Can you have a demo ready for testing in two weeks?"

"Yes, sir. I will conference my top engineers and planners now to start the project."

70

"Very good." Then Lieutenant Antonio hangs up. He then calls the White House press secretary, Amber. "Hello, this is Lieutenant, Secret Ops Commander Antonio. Do you know any underground news reporters in Moscow?"

"Yes."

"Here is what I need. I want news to spread that there is a certain rebel group in Russia plotting to assassinate President Khrushchev. Can you find a person who can do this?"

"Sure."

"This is dangerous. If you need help afterward, call this number. When the phone picks up, no one will speak; just say code gray ghost; help will find you."

"Yes, sir." Then Antonio hangs up.

Quintin, sitting in his office eating lunch and drinking hot tea, gets an encrypted call. He picks up. "Have you found the book yet?"

"No, sir, but I know who has it." Quintin pauses; the phone remains silent. "The president has it,"

The voice says, "Get it now! Find it! Send the cleaner to retrieve the book, and do not touch or open it!"

"How can I retrieve it if I can't touch it?"

"Use prongs and a lead-lined briefcase."

"Okay," Quintin replies and pulls himself together. He thinks to himself, "I need that book. But where would he keep it? The only way to find out is to have the president followed." He shakes off his nervousness and calls the cleaners.

The phone is picked up but there's no answer. "I have another job for you. This one is really dangerous," Quintin speaks first.

The cleaner smiles inwardly. It's about time we get a real challenge. These Americans think they know danger," The cleaner says, chuckling.

Quintin continues, "I need you to follow the President of America. And listen, if the Secret Service catches any of you, you're

71

dead. I can't help you. We're looking for a jet-black book with gold-green-edged pages inside. Do not touch or take it. Just get the precise location. This book is important to Khrushchev, so don't mess this up."

"Yes, sir."

The cleaners look up, hearing a knock on the door. A feminine voice spoke. "Body service."

Both cleaners look at each other, grinning. Then one says to the other. "Hey, the boss doesn't accept failure." He gives the ladies $1k to leave, then the cleaners pack up, check out, jump into the SUV and head out to follow the president and locate the Book of Ideology.

On the way back to DC, the cleaners call the encrypted phone. Quintin picked up and remained silent. Cleaner 1 says, "We're in DC at the Ritz Carlton on 31st and K Street." Quintin said, "Ok. He's been invited to a birthday party 3 days from now." The phone hangs up.

3 days later, while Cleaner 1 is joking with a hotel maid, an encrypted phone rings. Cleaner 2 picks up and remains silent. "The president's motorcade is heading home now. He will pass your position in 10 minutes."

Cleaner 2 tells cleaner 1. "We have work in 10 minutes," the maid, who smiles and says, "Call me," Then both cleaners grab their gear and run for the SUV to catch the passing motorcade.

There were 3 black Suburban, 2 state troopers, and 6 motorcycles. Michael's on the phone with Avienda. She says, "Michael, I appreciate you doing this. I know the risk you're taking,"

"Hey, relax. I said if you or Darien ever needed anything, just call."

Avienda responds, "I don't want your reputation ruined again because of me."

The cleaners in the black SUV go unnoticed by the Secret Service as they turn out of the hotel lot, 600 yards behind the trailing motorcade. No one paid attention to the long black SUV following. The motorcade turns right into the presidential estate. The cleaner drives past the next light, turn right, and circle around to the east side of the presidential estate, concealing the SUV from view.

Michael says, "I'm home," then hangs up with Avienda. He goes inside and tells the house staff, "No dinner. I'm going out tonight. Ready my black Imani suit with a gray-gold tie and gator snake wingtip shoes." The butler responds, "Right away, sir."

Michael thinks about the request to execute Khrushchev, the Russian president. He goes downstairs to browse through a book of ideology, takes the book out of the safe, and sits down at the coffee table, determined to make this work. The Secret Service starts to relax their guard, close to shift time inside the presidential estate. Four perimeter guards take shifts, 2 on, 2 off. Two hours before the shift change, on the east side, a guard takes a perimeter walk and sees nothing.

He says to the other guard, "I'm tired. Stayed up late watching the Miami Dolphins beat the crap out of the Washington Redskins 22 to 6. Won twelve hundred dollar bet, but, man, I'm sleepy."

The other guard responds, "I'm hungry. I missed lunch. We gotta have something to eat now. The first guard suggests, "Tell you what, if you can keep watch for 20 minutes, I'll run down to Subway and grab me an Italian chicken sub. On the way back, I can pick you up coffee from Starbucks," The second guard jokes, "Hey, don't fall asleep, or we'll be watching each other's butts in prison," The first guard reassures him, "I got it."

The guards take off, and the cleaner sees one guard leave. Cleaner 1 looks at Cleaner 2 and smiles, saying, "These American guards, unbelievable. In the KGB Secret Service, that's a death sentence." Cleaner 1 waits five minutes, saying, "Keep your eye on

Sleepy. I'll locate the book." Cleaner 1 jumps the concrete wall and runs back between hedges, checking each window for cameras and laser sensors. Following each window back, he comes to a basement window. Looking in carefully, he sees President Michael sitting with a black-covered book with gold-green edge pages. Cleaner 1 thinks, "Easiest job I've ever done."

Making his way back, he tells Cleaner 2, "I located the book." Cleaner 2 asks, "Where?" Cleaner 1 responds, "Downstairs, on the coffee table." Cleaner 2 then asks, "Hey, where's the guard?" Cleaner 1 looks around and sees the guard sleeping behind the south wall hedge. They both chuckle quietly. "Okay, make the call," Cleaner 1 says. They call in, "We've located the book."

Quintin, excited, says, "Ok, get the book." Cleaner 1 looks up and says, "What?" Just then, the first guard returns, walking the perimeter until he sees the second guard sleeping. He walks up quietly and kicks his feet out from under him. The second guard bangs his head against the concrete wall, whimpering in pain. The first guard says, "I see you're still awake. That's good. Here's your coffee. If anything happens to the president, we'll both be in prison."

"Trying not to be Sambo body boys, Quintin," the cleaner says. Quintin responds, "Ok." He grabs the led-lined briefcase and prongs to recover the book. "Yes, the briefcases and prongs are in the SUV. We need time. The first guard is back on duty as he starts his perimeter walk. Cleaner 2 hangs up quietly, gets in the van, and drives off, circling the block. He comes back, seeing the Secret Service motorcade back with lots of commotion. Everyone is at attention. A few minutes later, President Michael leaves the estate, and the entire Secret Service and guards leave at the same time.

Lieutenant Antonio devises a shift rotation route so the presidential estate would always be guarded from the inside out with special access tunnels. The cleaners can't believe their luck.

They wait about 10 minutes, parking at the east wall, concealing the SUV. They grab their equipment, jump the concrete wall, and carefully move between hedges to the south basement window. Cleaner 1 peeks in and says, "Hey, there's no book on the coffee table."

Cleaner 2 goes in, saying, "It's got to be here," and starts searching inside for a hidden place. They uncover a fireplace safe. Being expert thieves, in 6 minutes, Cleaner 1 pops the safe. Cleaner 2 grins until his cheeks hurt, grabs the book with prongs and places it in the led-lined briefcase.

The guards coming on duty see the silent alarm, check hidden cameras, and see the two men in the basement room. Quietly, they surround the estate, hitting the Russian cleaners with stun guns and handcuffing them when they come out. President Michael gets a call informing him, "Sir, we apprehended two thieves breaking into your estate. They have a lead briefcase."

"Ok, take them to Secret Service headquarters and put them in the interrogation room. I'm on my way."

"Yes, sir." The caller confirms. Michael tells the driver to turn around and go to Secret Service Headquarters, then calls Avienda. "Avienda, I'm really sorry. Something very important came up. I can't make it. I promise I'll make up to you."

"Ok."

Michael arrives at headquarters, and the Secret Service briefs him, "We have 2 Russians in the interrogation room. We confiscated a lead briefcase. No one opened it. Waiting for your orders, sir."

"Ok, good. Show me this briefcase," Michael says, "Here, in room 2."

"Ok, you may go," Michael dismisses him. Michael opens the briefcase to find the Book of Ideology and the set of prongs. He thinks to himself, "So that's what they were looking for."

Thinking quickly, he exchanges his personal diary for the book of ideology, closes the briefcase, and calls Lieutenant Antonio. "I have a special job for you. Come to Secret Service headquarters. I have two Russians in custody. There's a briefcase with my personal diary in it. I need you to make a counterfeit book with a jet-black cover and gold-green edge pages. Exchange it for the diary. Give the Secret Service authorization to let the Russians go. These guys must have connections in high places. That way, whoever sent them won't know their plan has been compromised."

Once Lieutenant Antonio finishes the president's task with the counterfeit book, Antonio glances at his watch. It's almost time for the NASA project demonstration. He heads home, takes a shower, and gets dressed. At 0300, he pulls into the NASA special project complex. The special project manager invites him in for the project demo. Being top-secret, only two people were present: the project manager and the top operation engineer, explaining the demo.

"What we have here is a man-made meteor composed of real meteor rock from outer space. Inside this basketball-sized rock are three carbon composite smaller meteors protecting special mechanic devices," the engineer explains.

"The first device is a 1-inch diameter air distractor. The second device is the same size with two curved, snake-like steel teeth able to inject real snake venom. The third device is 1.4 inches in diameter because of the extra power needed to penetrate the brain and fire electroshock to paralyze speech and eyesight. We were not able to find a single power source to fly 50 miles, but we did install an advanced super smell solar array able to power flight for 10 miles per night."

The engineer activates a test on a sleeping pig, and all three devices work flawlessly. "The plan is once the meteor reaches 250 miles into outer space, it will be released, falling to Earth and reaching speeds of 17,000 miles per hour, catching fire and imitating a meteor. At 8000 feet above ground, the meteor will blow apart. The three small devices capable of surviving impact will self-activate. The protective shield will open, turning on a miniature camera and laser perimeter detection sensor. Then, it will raise the solar array. They will keep track of each other through a friend or foe beacon. The entire plan has already been programmed into a fire-and-forget smart chip."

"Ok, gentlemen, good job. Prepare for execution. You will be contacted via encrypted code word deniability. If you don't receive a second encrypted code before 0300, proceed as planned. This never happened. Understood?" Lieutenant instructs.

The lieutenant goes home, calls the special ops team, and lets them know stage 1 is ready for execution. He calls President Michael on the encrypted phone, informing him, "Your request is ready to be activated."

"Ok, stand by," thinking about Avienda and how he can make up for last night. He calls her, saying, "Hello, this is Michael. Are you free for dinner tonight? I have some news you might like" Avienda hesitates, then decides, "Yes, I'm free."

"Ok, I will send a limousine to pick you up."

"Where are we going?" she asks. It's a surprise. Trust me," says Michael.

When she arrives at the airport, the president's Air Force One private plane is waiting with the Secret Service to help her board the plane. Michael smiles, greeting her and ordering the pilot to take off. Once reaching cruising altitude, waiters come out and set the table for two. Avienda is impressed. After some small talk, Michael says, "You remember I told you and the American people we would avenge President Thomas' death? Well, the Russian president is about to be assassinated."

Avienda looks into Michael's eyes, feeling relief and something else. Not sure what it was, they finished dinner and sightseeing. Returning, a limousine is waiting to take her home. "Michael, thank you for this," Avienda says.

Chapter 8

Road To Redemption

Michael awoke to thunder and dark clouds outside his window, glancing over at his alarm clock—only 6:15 am. He flicked on the TV to the news channel CNN Weather Report. Hurricane Dorian was approaching South Florida as a Category 5 hurricane, with 185 mph winds extending 175 miles wide, stalled over the Grand Bahamas Islands. A hurricane advisory alert was issued for the next 48 hours. A butler knocked on his bedroom door.

"Sir, would you like coffee and your usual lemon-lime Danish?"

"Yes, come in,"

Michael is thinking to himself, "Just what I need to chase this déjà vu feeling away."

Four years ago today, President Thomas was assassinated. Determined to make Khrushchev remember and regret his evil deed, Michael picked up the encrypted phone and called Lieutenant, saying, "It's a go; activate the plan."

"Yes, sir, Mr. President."

Michael hung up. Lieutenant called NASA.

"Hello, this is NASA's special project manager," he hears one word code. "Deniability."

Antonio, hanging up the call, "Special ops team, meet me in Situation Room 0300. We have a green light for operation at 0300 sharp."

All special ops members were there and ready to deploy anywhere necessary. Lieutenant Antonio:

"Gentlemen, the president requests this plan be activated now. We need three teams: one at NASA monitoring deployment for unauthorized communication and surveillance, team two tracking military advisor Quintin's whereabouts during operation, and team three providing special protection details for President Michael in case of a retaliatory strike."

Antonio looked at each ops commander. "Any questions?"

"No, sir."

"Okay, let's get it done."

At 0300, the NASA space station's special project engineer supervised the final test and loading of a special military project onto the space starship. The starship lifted off without any problems, heading for the International Space Station. Halfway to the space station, a man-made meteor was released, with all ops teams in place. They detected no unauthorized communication or surveillance. The lieutenant received a call confirming the first stage was complete—the meteor was falling on target, reaching speeds upwards of 17,000 miles per hour. Team 1 detected Russian radar tracking the meteor but found no unusual communications or tracking transmissions. The meteor hit the atmosphere, glowing bright gold-green. At 8,000 feet, the meteor broke into three pieces, impacting the ground at 400 mph. Everyone in NASA Special Operations awaited the activation signal, confirming the device survived the impact. Eighteen minutes later, the device transmitted the activation code. The lieutenant received a call confirming the second stage was complete.

Khrushchev is in a secret bunker, planning a massive invasion against Ukraine, Poland, Germany, France, and Spain. Thinking to himself, "This will make Hitler's invasion look like McDonald's reverie." Grinning, "The book of ideology is on its way back, and I'll have no problem convincing the Russian generals the time is right while the Americans are weak."

A security officer comes in and whispers to the Russian president, "We've received news about an assassination attempt

80

that will be made on your life by a Russian rebel group."

Khrushchev gets up, "Gentlemen, excuse me. We'll need to cut this short."

Stepping outside the meeting room, Khrushchev requests double elite bodyguards. Then he goes to his private office and turns on the TV to a Russian news reporter speaking live, "We have just received a report from a religious zealot group vowing to assassinate President Khrushchev."

Three hours later, elite guards bring Khrushchev an envelope wrapped around a rock thrown over the compound wall written in Russian. It reads, "Remember, you broadcast live; all weakness must be eradicated." "No, Mr. President, all evil must be eradicated," the message continues. "We stand for the sanctity of all life, and in three weeks, you will be where you belong, Mr. President."

Two weeks before lieutenant asked Amber to put out the word about President Khrushchev's pending assassination to ensure fear and maximum stress

Terrell was staying at a safe house with nothing to do. He decided to ask one of the Secret Service guards how they got into the Secret Service. "Ka'Juan, do you have any military or special forces training?"

"No,"

"You need some special military or law enforcement training with top-secret clearance."

"Ah, man, I don't have any experience."

The next day, Quintin visited the safe house, remembering that the cleaner had mentioned three other names along with Kathie during their interrogation. Ka'Juan, Quintin's inside connection in the Secret Service, reveal the witness protection safe house location. Quintin was plotting an accidental death for all three to ensure no witnesses, but luck was on his side as the guard Terrell was speaking with was Quintin's inside connection. The one name Terrell was asking about how to join the Secret Service detail.

Quintin thought he could cozy up to Terrell and turn him into an informant. The guard introduced Quintin to Terrell, "Hey, this is the military advisor to the president."

Terrell extended his hand, "Nice to meet you, sir."

"None of that. We're all on the same team. A friend of the president is a friend of mine."

Terrell smiling, "I was asking how to become a Secret Service agent."

Quintin thinking to himself, "Yes. He could be my eyes and ears inside micheal's enter circle. Do you have any experience?"

"No." Terrell looked down.

Quintin smiled, "Don't worry, we can get around this. Just call it on-the-job training. Let me make a few calls." Terrell looked up, smiling big, "Okay, oh man, this is great! Thank you, sir."

"I'll have Ka'Juan bring you by my office tomorrow. We can talk then,".

"Yes, sir,".

"Keep this between us," Quintin left, returning to his office. He called up his White House personal aide, "I need temporary top-secret clearance documents and a badge for Terrell. He's in the White House protection witness program."

"Yes, sir," the aide responded.

The next day, Ka'Juan brought Terrell to see Quintin. "Have a seat, Terrell," as he handed him his new Secret Service ID badge, a special agent Glock 19, Gen5 MOS with forward slide serrations, AmeriGlo Bold night sights, a Streamlight TLR-7A weapon light. Terrell's eyes went big, his mouth fell open, and he grinned with excitement. Quintin smiled back.

"Did you know the reporter Kathie Nail?"

"No, I didn't. Lina knew her,"

82

"Who is Lina?"

"She used to be a news reporter,"

"How did you meet her?"

"Darian and I were investigating his father's death."

"Who is Darian's father?"

"President Thomas. His assassination was on the news, and his brother Jonathan was also murdered."

"Did you find out who did it?"

"We know who killed President Thomas, but we are investigating why. We have some ideas. Lina is helping us with research," Terrell explained but then stopped talking, thinking to himself, "Be careful. He's asking too many questions. I don't want to get Darian and Lina in trouble."

Quintin noticed Terrell's hesitation. "Okay, let's get your training started. Ka'Juan will be your trainer."

"Okay, great."

Quintin called Ka'Juan to his office. "You'll be training Terrell."

"Yes, sir."

Terrell grabbed his equipment and followed Ka'Juan out.

The cleaners caught a plane back to Moscow with the led-lined briefcase, arriving at 0100 Russian time. They were met by Khrushchev's KGB elite guard and taken straight to the secret underground bunker. Khrushchev received a call that the briefcase had arrived.

"Take the briefcase to my private office and guard it until I arrive."

"Yes, sir."

The cleaners were then sent to the guard quarters until they were needed.

Quintin's encrypted phone rang. Picking up, he remained silent. "The briefcase has arrived." The phone hung up.

Quintin sat back, smiling, thinking about his payment and maybe a bonus. Later that evening, Khrushchev walked to his private office and asked the guard, "Is the briefcase secure?"

"Yes, sir."

"Okay, you may leave."

"Yes, sir."

Khrushchev went into his office excitedly, sat down, and opened the briefcase. He saw the book of ideology, smiled, kissed it, and then opened it, thinking, "Now I will rule the world," and laughed maniacally. Suddenly, he noticed something about the book, stopped laughing, and started shaking with rage. "This is not the book of ideology!"

Grabbing his Makarov pistol, he ran to the office door, opened it, and shot the guard in the back of the head before he could turn. Running back to his desk, he grabbed the phone and called the elite guard. "Bring the two cleaners now!" "Yes, sir." slamming down the phone, breathing hard.

The cleaners arrived in 3 minutes. Khrushchev, with a pistol in hand, asked the cleaners, "Where did you get this book?"

"From the American president's house, downstairs, on the coffee table," one cleaner said, shaking with fear as he saw Khrushchev's rage boiling over.

"I will ask you one time what happened, and you will tell me everything, because this is not the book."

"Okay, we jumped concrete wall and went back to basement window. The book was not on table. So, we searched and found his safe. Then we broke in, took the book with prongs just like you ordered and put it in briefcase. We didn't touch it but umm.." The cleaner hesitated.

Khrushchev shot the cleaner point blank, then looked at the second cleaner calmly.

"You may continue now."

"Okay, guards were waiting. We got captured and taken to Secret Service headquarters, detained for 4 hours, then let go. We thought Quintin had pulled some strings to get us released."

"What happened to the briefcase while you were being detained?"

"It was confiscated and returned when they released us,"

Khrushchev smiled. "Good, you may go."

"Yes, sir, thank you, sir."

As the cleaners turned to go, Khrushchev nodded to the elite guards. The cleaner walking out of the office was executed by the elite guard with one shot to the head. Calming down, Khrushchev called Quintin on the encrypted phone. He didn't want Quintin to know he knew about the counterfeit book. He said, "Good job," and hung up. Quintin was relieved that it was over.

One month earlier, Rebecca, Quintin's sister-in-law, was visiting his sister while Quintin and Derek were discussing extra work. "Hey, I'll be retiring next week from the military. If you have any jobs you need handled, call me."

"As a matter of fact, I have something you can help me with."

"Okay, what?"

"Jonathan, the former president's son, the people like him so much they elected him president. But this guy is too righteous."

"What's the problem with that?"

"See, that's it. You can't rule unless you're willing to step on some people."

"Okay, so what do you need?"

"In three weeks, I need you to make him disappear without a trace."

"Okay. How much is this job paying?"

"250 million."

"Wait, what?" Quintin chuckled, knowing he got Derek's attention. "Okay, brother, when do you want this done?"

85

"You and your team meet me in DC in two weeks."

"No, I work alone. That way, no loose ends."

"Okay, understood. See you then. Thanks."

"No, thank you. And I thought retirement would be boring." Rebecca's heart beat fast as she left the bathroom. She told Derek's sister that something had come up and she had to leave immediately. On the way back to the hotel, she called the airport for an early flight back to DC, not knowing her family relatives were so dangerous.

Rebecca worked as the press secretary for Michael. She had just gotten the position three months ago and really liked it. Her last two weeks had been exciting. Every time she gave her press release, this wavy-haired guy with hazel-brown eyes would stare at her like he knew her. He didn't look like a reporter; he had the aura of power.

"Why is he here?" Rebecca thought once she finished. She grabbed her notes, hurrying to leave, but spilled papers everywhere, feeling embarrassed as she started picking them up. She heard a voice say,

"Hey, need some help?"

Without a reply, he helped pick up the papers, making it look easy. Before she could get five sheets, he was done.

"Here you go. My name is Darien. And you are?"

"Rebecca. Thanks."

"Hey, would you like to get some coffee?" Looking around and hesitating, then saw his visitor badge marked "President VIP."

"Okay, sure."

The next night, the lieutenant gave the okay to proceed with stage 3. NASA's special engineer activated all three drones to fly to waypoint 1 in stealth mode. Two hours later, the drones shut down 10 miles closer to Moscow's secret bunker. The lieutenant received an encrypted call, "Third stage complete."

After a full day of solar charge, the drones flew to the last waypoint before entering the secret bunker compound. The lieutenant advised the president of the operation status. Michael gave the okay to proceed. The lieutenant messaged the NASA special ops engineer to activate the drone to fly just outside the secret bunker compound wall at waypoint 2 atop the searchlight tower for maximum surveillance reconnaissance. Two hours later, the signal of the waypoint position was received. The infrared camera activated, and the lieutenant received the call, "Stage 4 complete."

The lieutenant called the president, "Sir, we're at the point of no return. Your call, sir."

"Execute."

The lieutenant called NASA back, giving the green light. The next night, the NASA special ops engineer instructed the drone to activate pre-programmed smart chip mode. The rest of the operation would be carried out autonomously. The drone activated the auto motion sensor locator as guards were en route to the target. Then drone activated camouflage mode, flying and attaching to a guard's Kalashnikov rifle, blending to conceal from the compound's high-tech array sensor. From this point, no signal could be sent or received. The special ops team and NASA special engineer would have to wait until the operation was complete and the drone escaped the compound. Elite guards were heading to receive commands from Khrushchev for invasion mobilization. The guards arrived at Khrushchev's private office, knocked on the door, and heard, "Come in."

The drone detached from the Kalashnikov rifle, flying onto an object in the office, blending in. The Smart programming sensor probe confirmed the target. Khrushchev told the elite guard, "Have all generals here at 0800 tomorrow."

"Yes, sir," He left to carry out the order.

Khrushchev called the two remaining cleaners in the United

States, "Kidnap the military advisor Quintin. Take him to an abandoned building and call me. I have hard questions for him."

"Understood. Yes, sir," the phone hung up, and the cleaner grinned with excitement.

That night, as Khrushchev watched the 10 PM news, the drone activated its final instructions for execution. The TV was on; elite guards were on duty. The lieutenant instructed, "Let him know death is coming." The first drone turned off stealth mode, flying off the lampshade at full speed. Khrushchev heard a sound like a mosquito; the drone flew right up to his face, ejecting fog-like powder, extracting all oxygen from the air, leaving only CO_2.

Khrushchev tried to scream, but before he could, second drones flew off the wall at full speed. With snake-like steel teeth, hitting his jugular vein just below his left ear. The third drone flew off the opposite wall at full speed, extending a hypodermic needle electrically charged to interrupt sight and motor function, flying into Khrushchev's right ear, penetrating his skull and brain's optic nerves, causing blindness and paralyzing movement. In disbelief, he heard President Michael's voice, "Some people mistake kindness for weakness; Americans are not weak. We value the sanctity of life. Only the creator has total supremacy over who lives and who dies. But you were right about one thing: all weakness must be eradicated. You just misunderstood his meaning. All evil must be eradicated. So please, stop crying and go where you belong." Khrushchev's last thought was, "Thomas, please, I'm—" Then blackness.

When the drone's sensor confirmed no pulse, all three retracted from Khrushchev's body and returned to camouflage, awaiting the retreat operation. At 0800, the elite guard returned to inform the Russian president that the generals were waiting in the situation room. Knocking on the office door and hearing no response, the elite guard entered and saw the president sitting up, watching the news. Going over to Khrushchev and facing him, the elite guard, knowing what death looked like, felt his hair stand on end with fear and ran out pulling the alarm. While the alarm was sounding, All three drones escaped undetected in the chaos before the compound locked down. The drones retreated to transmit waypoints, sending encrypted video and audio data to confirm mission success. Over the next five nights, the drones traveled and reached the Volkhov River in Novgorod. Flying over the river, they self-destructed, leaving no trace.

The two remaining Russian cleaners in the United States kidnapped Quintin, pretending to need orders. They called his encrypted phone; Quintin picked up but remained silent. The cleaner asked, "What's your order, sir?"

"Now that the book is back in Russia, stay put. I may still have work for you."

The cleaner, surmising from the background noise, realized Quintin was at his DC office. They drove to his office and bugged his car, and Quintin, unaware, Khrushchev knew about the counterfeit book. He still planned to cozy up to Terrell to get information to bring Michael down and become president, creating an alliance with Khrushchev. Quintin felt relaxed and in charge for once, leaving the office early and heading downtown for a massage. The cleaners tracked him and arrived at the massage parlor. Quintin, smiling, went in and spent four hours there. When he came out, it was dark, and not many people were around. The cleaners drove up beside Quintin while he was walking to his car, grabbed him, and hit him with pistol butt, knocking him out before throwing him into the SUV and taking off. The lieutenant of the special ops observed this and called in Antonio. Antonio informed President Michael, who told Antonio to just observe and keep audio record for now. The cleaners took Quintin to an abandoned building out of town, where he was tied to a chair. Quintin came awake, realizing he was bound, and looked up, fully awake.

"What's the meaning of this?"

"You work for me." The cleaner smiled.

"The boss wants to speak with you." Quintin, thinking of Khrushchev, cursed him as a double-crossing communist scum, wondering why he would do this after all the work he had done. The cleaner tried calling Khrushchev's encrypted phone, but it rang and rang with no answer, so they hung up.

1 hour later, the cleaner's phone rang. He answered, and it was Khrushchev's elite guard commander. "The Russian president has been assassinated," the commander said. The cleaner, in disbelief, hung up and looked at his partner.

"The boss is dead."

Quintin jerked his head up, and they both looked at him, suspecting his involvement. They began interrogating him, starting with a hammer to the kneecap. Quintin started screaming, spilling everything he knew. The ops team informed Antonio and Michael about the ongoing interrogation. President Michael said, "Let it continue."

Quintin cried like a baby. "I don't know anymore."

"You're lying."

"No, I'm telling the truth."

"For each lie, one toe will be smashed."

"Please, no." Finally, Quintin revealed his involvement in President Jonathan's death.

"Okay, okay, I paid Derek to make Jonathan disappear." The cleaners looked at each other in shock.

"He's a killer too," they laughed.

"I like this guy." Quintin smiled, thinking he might get out of this.

The cleaner looked back at Quintin, laughing, "Hey, we'll make it quick," and brought two more hammers to finish quickly.

Once Quintin died, the ops team informed Antonio and Michael about Quintin's confession.

"Justice is served."

The cleaners took Quintin's body to New York and stuffed it into a sewer manhole. The ops team tracked the cleaner, awaiting orders.

The cleaners finished their job and caught a private plane heading back to Russia. The ops team informed the lieutenant, and Antonio ordered the cleaners to be eliminated and not to leave any evidence.

"Yes, sir."

The ops team called the SR72 Darkstar, which was on standby and gave the green light to eliminate the crew and the plane heading to Russia.

"Roger."

The SR72 Darkstar swung around, hitting full afterburner and reaching supersonic speed in 3.2 seconds. The America elite fighter jet reached Mach 6 in 5 seconds, flying so fast that the crew onboard the private plane didn't see anything but heard a sonic boom. The plane exploded, leaving no trace.

Rebecca and Darien continued meeting for coffee talks and became more trusting. After two weeks, Rebecca talked about her sister and how she loved reporting but was tortured and murdered. Darien asked what her name was.

"Kathie."

"I know your sister and how she died." Rebecca went cold inside, staring at Darien in shock, and he went silent. Rebecca looked down into her coffee cup, thinking, "Oh God, I can finally know the truth."

Looking back up to Darien, "Will you tell me the truth? Don't leave anything out."

Darien agreed.

"Yes, let's go somewhere private, and I will tell you everything."

After Darien explained about Kathie, Lina, Terrell, and his father's death, he mentioned his brother Jonathan's death and how he disappeared before being found in a sewer manhole in New York. Rebecca realized and said, "He was the president after your father, right and his vice president was Quintin,"

"Yes."

Rebecca looked down.

"What is it?"

"I might know who murdered your brother."

"What? Wait, tell me what you know, please,"

Rebecca recounted the conversation she overheard between Quintin and Derek, Quintin's brother, about extra work and making someone disappear for $250 million. Darien felt a mix of anger, rage, and love churning inside him. He felt protective of Rebecca, making sure she got home safely, thinking, "Finally, retribution for my brother's honor."

He left to call Terrell and Lina.

"We need to talk. Meet in Michael's private office."

Darien called his mother, "Can you and Michael meet with me tomorrow? I have some important news."

"Yes, okay, son. What time?"

"Noon tomorrow."

The next day, Darien, Rebecca, Terrell, Lina, Avienda, President Michael, and Lieutenant Antonio all met in Michael's private conference room. Michael spoke first.

"Darien. Avienda and I have been talking about your dad, President Thomas, and my part in stealing the book from him by courting Avienda when she was vulnerable. I knew this was wrong; I was craving power and prestige. But I assure you, I would never conspire or consent to your father's death. Now, to make up for my part in your father's death, if you run for president, I'll willingly step down to ensure victory and turn over the book that rightfully belongs to you. And I ask your consent to marry Avienda."

She looked up at Michael, seeing he meant it, and everyone was shocked into silence. Michael looked at his lieutenant and nodded. Antonio stood up.

"Ladies and gentlemen, I have recorded evidence that will answer your questions about Quintin and Derek conspiring to murder Jonathan and Quintin conspiring with Khrushchev to tarnish Michael's reputation and return the book to Russian President Khrushchev. Also, Quintin, the military advisor, has been found in a New York sewer manhole."

He was murdered by Russian cleaners, the same people who murdered the reporter Kathie Nail. We tracked the Russians on a private plane heading back to Russia and eliminated them. Michael looked up and saw that Rebecca couldn't take much more, nodding at Lieutenant to stop there. Terrell spoke up after hearing what Quintin did. He confessed to asking Quintin to help him join the Secret Service and how he told Quintin some things about Darien and Lina.

Darien and Lina both looked at him, wondering what he said. Darien stared at him, and Terrell knew what Darien wanted to know. Terrell shook his head no.

"Lina, I'm sorry, I didn't know." She looked away, tightening her jaw. Darien looked up toward Michael's lieutenant, remembering Derek, "What do we do about Derek?"

Then, turning to Rebecca, "He's your relative. What do you want?"

"I don't know. He murdered your brother."

Antonio spoke up. "I have an idea. We'll put out a wanted bulletin on him, scaring him to make a run for it, intentionally allowing him to escape. This means he can never return to America again without facing life in prison."

Lieutenant Antonio looked over at the president. Michael turned to Darien. Darien turned to Rebecca. "Is this okay for you?"

She nodded.

"Okay."

Michael turned back to the lieutenant. "Okay, make it happen."

"Yes, sir." Antonio left the room.

Later that evening, Derek was eating dinner. He used his cell phone to check his bank account in the Cayman Islands, saw his balance, and smiled. Calling his wife from the living room sofa, he said, "Hey, bring me some hot coffee."

"Okay."

Derek, still watching for a good action movie, flipped through the channels. He saw the news, about to change channels, when something caught his eye. His wife brought his coffee. "Here you go."

"Thanks, babe."

"You're welcome."

Still watching the news, a reporter announced, "We have breaking news live. President's military advisor Quintin's body has just been found in a New York sewer manhole. In the same New York area, in the past four years, two other bodies have been found, including former President Jonathan, the son of President Thomas, who was assassinated by Russian President Khrushchev."

Derek was still riveted to the TV and started drinking his coffee. The news reporter continued, "The White House lieutenant, Antonio, just put out a press release statement. They have evidence on the suspect involved in former President Jonathan's death. His name is Derek, a former military retired Navy SEAL. There's a wanted bulletin out for his arrest."

Derek spilled his coffee, cursed, and jumped up. His wife asked, "What's wrong?"

"Nothing."

Derek thought, "She doesn't know; I've got to keep this a secret."

Still in pain from spilling hot coffee, he heard the authorities say the suspect lives in Reevesville, South Carolina.

Derek's eyes widened. "What the..."

"What, babe?"

Derek smiled, "You know what I think we need? A vacation. Let's go to the Cayman Islands."

His wife smiled back. "For real?"

"Yes, and start packing now; we're leaving tonight."

"But I need time to pack."

"No, just one suitcase. I'll buy everything in the Cayman Islands."

"You promise?"

"Yes, let's go. Let me call my friend to let her know where I'm going."

"No, you can call from there."

Derek called his military buddy.

"Hello, this is Derek."

"Hey, I need to call in that favor."

"Yeah, sure."

"I need documents, passports, and licenses for two people and a private jet to the Cayman Islands. No paper trail."

"Okay, sure, no problem. Thanks."

Team 2 Ops were already at Derek's address, monitoring.

"Call the lieutenant. He's making a run for it."

"Let him run. He'll leave America's soil. If he wasn't one of us, I would eliminate him."

Chapter 9

Inner Struggle

Darien was dreaming, sitting at the dining room table, waiting for Mom to bring dinner for Dad, Jonathan, and him. Dad was talking to Jonathan. "Son, don't think about what you want. Always put God first. Sometimes people think being first gives you the right to have more. No. God's always first, Jonathan."

"I don't understand."

"Darien, are you listening?"

"Yes, sir."

"Jonathan, if you trust the Creator and yourself, you will have peace in everything you do. Never ask yourself, 'What should I do?' Look inward, He's there,"

"Okay, but..." Dad smiled, "Don't worry, son. In time, He will answer."

"Darien, son, are you hearing me?"

"Yes, sir,"

Darien's mind was outside in the sprinkling rain.

Behind him, he smelled food cooking.

"It's almost ready. Go wash your hands." He hears chairs moving but he couldn't move or turn away from the window.

There was a woodpecker in the hedges, flying back and forth, picking off bugs. It flies on the window seal, and looked at him, then started pecking on the glass. "Is this a dream? Dad and Jonathan are dead."

Mom calls Darien. "Are you getting up today?" He opened his eyes. It was a dream. He hears a knocking, like something hitting glass. He sat up and looked toward the bedroom window. Through

96

parted curtains, he saw the same woodpecker pecking on the glass. It stopped, looked at him, pecked three more times, and flew off.

He hears Mom call again.

"I'm up."

"Your food is ready."

"Okay, thanks, Mom."

Darien gets up, goes to the dining room, and sits down, praying before eating breakfast. He's thinking to himself, "What's happening to me?" After he finished eating, he heads downstairs to the den and pulls out the Book of Truth, looking for answers. He remembers Edwin's instructions: turn the book over and concentrating on the back cover. Words begin to appear. "Michael's actions assassinate Khrushchev. The book remains with Michael." He thinks, "I know this." More words begin to appear. "Darien, the American president's actions build a safe haven city, solving border problems and brokering peace between Ukraine and Russia." Darien sees these words, which frighten him, losing concentration. He feels chills all over and senses something behind him. He turns quickly, seeing no one, and puts the book back, breathing hard from the supernatural, unknown experience. He goes upstairs outside for fresh air and to clear his thoughts. The sky is cloudy, the wind blowing, tree branches waving, and the smell of ozone in the air, the kind just after a lightning strike. Then a voice speaks in his mind.

"It's time."

Darien knows what this means; he needs no more convincing. This is his time, like his father and Jonathan. It's time to step up to destiny. Falling asleep completely that night, he awakens feeling changed, confident in his purpose.

To set America on the true path of integrity, he is calling Michael. "Hello, Darien, how are you doing, son?" "Okay, I guess. I need to know all you know about the Book of Ideology." "Okay. When would you like to meet?" "This weekend if you have time."

"Okay, yes. I told you and your mother just ask, and I'll make time."

"Okay, thanks. See you this weekend, Saturday evening, at the presidential estate for privacy."

Darien met Michael alone, not sure about Terrell after the betrayal to Quintin. Michael let the guards know he would have a guest coming over. When Darien arrived, the guards let him in.

"No problem, Mr. Darien, go right in; you're cleared, no pass needed."

Parking his BMW in the roundabout driveway, he got out and rang the doorbell. The butler opened the door.

"Right this way, Mr. Darien."

He led Darien through a long atrium hallway, down curved stairs to a large library guest waiting room.

"Please, have a seat. Would you like any refreshments?"

"No, just water."

"Very good, I will bring it right away, sir. The president is on his way. Please avail yourself of this room's amenities."

Two minutes later, the butler returned with filtered water.

"Thank you." Darien walked around, reading book labels.

Michael walked in. "Hello, Darien, good to see you."

"Thank you for inviting me."

"We should get started; come with me."

Darien followed Michael to a secret room behind a wall bookshelf. After passing through the door, it automatically closed behind Darien. Michael turned. "I know it's a bit much, but you can never be too careful." He went to the fireplace, touching seven bricks like dialing a phone number. The coffee table flipped over, revealing a microwave-sized high-tech safe. Michael stood in front of the safe; a green light scanned his body and eye retina, then the safe clicked open. Darien was not one to be impressed.

"This is impressive."

Michael took the Book of Ideology out. The safe automatically closed and flipped back to the coffee table position.

"Okay, have a seat, Darien. Now I will explain everything I know about the Book of Ideology."

Darien and Michael were in secret for two hours. When they finished, Darien thought about telling Michael about the Book of Truth but remembered what happened to his father and changed his mind.

"It's yours."

"What?"

"The book, it's yours, take it."

"I will, but not yet. It's better if you keep it for now. You're still the president."

"Okay, when you're ready, it's here."

"Son, I want to help you by cleaning out as much corruption as possible before I step down. So if you need anything, just ask. I'm sorry I dishonored your dad's legacy."

"I can see you're changing; that means a lot, thank you," Darien left.

The next day, Darien goes to meet Terrell. "We need to talk."

"How long have we been friends, Terrell?"

"Okay, I know I messed up. Brother, can you forgive me? I got too close to power. It felt unbelievable. I can't explain. I thought it was worth anything to have this spotlight. I sold my soul, but now I know the soul is a lot more than money, power, and fame. It's honor, integrity, and doing what is right. I'm sorry. Give me another chance to make it right."

Darien looked Terrell in the eyes. After one whole minute, he nodded. "Okay, brother, let's fix America," they both smiled.

"I talked with Michael; he told me everything about the Book of Ideology."

"Hey, why didn't you take me?" Darien looked up, Terrell started laughing, and Darien laughed too.

"Okay, he's back, just like old times. Okay, now business. I've decided to run for president in the next election."

Terrell saw that Darien was serious, stopped laughing, and nodded, "Okay."

One year later

President Darien gives his inaugural speech. "Ladies and gentlemen, people of America, I am honored to be elected president of this free country. I promise to hold this privileged duty with the utmost esteem, knowing the past year has been a struggle with trying hardships. God gave us His most valuable privileges. Now, I endeavor to let prosperity reach all American citizens, leaving no one behind. Remember, our ancestors fought and died for this country. I will strive for peace, inject innovation, respect, and stability for all to their sacrifice. We the people must choose: man's ideology or the truth's. People, I will show you the truth, but it's up to you to accept."

"Edwin, I elect you as White House advisor. Terrell, I elect you as Secret Service director. Rebecca, I appoint you as press secretary. Lieutenant Antonio, I elect you as top military commander and head of Ghost Ops. Chappell, thank you for becoming my vice president. Okay, if everyone agrees, let's meet tomorrow at 0800 in my office to plan America's future. Terrell, have the Secret Service bring the motorcade. I'm going to Michael's estate to retrieve the Book of Ideology, and then I'll go to Mom's to pick up the Book of Truth."

"Terrell, what are you planning?"

"I will see what happens when both books are together."

"Hey, can I be there?"

"Not this time," Darien left.

He called Michael. "Hello."

"How's everything going, Mr. President?"

"Good. I'm on my way to pick up the book. Is this okay?"

"Sure. I'll be there in 30 minutes."

Darien retrieved the Book of Ideology and then went to his mom's to pick up the Book of Truth before returning to the White House. Walking into the Oval Office, he closed the 8-foot-tall double titanium doors behind him. He turned around, took 5 steps forward, stopped, then took 3 steps left and 1 step back. Turning right, he took 9 steps forward, then bent down and placed his right palm on the floor tile. A 4 by 4 tube lifted up, and Darien entered with both books in his briefcase. The tube sank into the floor, descending into a secret room under the United States bald eagle floor portrait in the center of the Oval Office, which ex-President Michael had built for storing the Book of Ideology. Darien set down his briefcase, opened it, and removed both books. He reviewed Edwin's instructions for the Book of Truth and Michael's instructions for the Book of Ideology, hesitating for 30 minutes while pondering what to do next.

Finally, he opened the Book of Ideology, then turned over the Book of Truth. He concentrated on the Book of Truth while falling into a dream trance. He found himself sitting at the dining room table, hearing Jonathan and his father, Thomas, talking.

"Son, you can build a border safe haven city to help immigrants while they are waiting for citizenship."

Darien thought in his mind, "What about terrorists?" but Jonathan and his father couldn't hear him. Darien woke from the dream, saw the Ideology book flipping pages, and words appeared on the Book of Truth, revealing all he needed to carry out his ideas and plans. Once again, he felt someone behind him and turned quickly, seeing no one. He put the books in separate cases in the safe, then left the secret room, walking out to the White House garden to get some fresh air and collect his thoughts.

The next morning at 0800, Darien received a call from the White House secretary. "Mr. President, your 8 o'clock guests are here."

"Okay, thanks, Miss Pearl." Darien, hanging up, walked to the Oval Office meeting. He saw everyone was there and spoke, "Sorry, I stayed up late planning. Would anyone like coffee or donuts?"

"Mr. Edwin?"

"Coffee, thanks,"

"Lieutenant?"

"Nothing, sir. Thanks,"

"Rebecca?"

"Ginger tea, thank you,"

"Mr. Chappell?"

"Water, please. Thanks,"

"Terrell?"

"Two cake donuts, one cherry-filled, one glazed donut, coffee, and Evian bottled water. Thanks,"

Darien stared at Terrell, shaking his head, then turned to Lina. "Just hot cocoa, if you have it. Thank you."

Darien walked to his desk and pressed the intercom.

"Miss Pearl, have the butler bring these refreshments right away."

"Yes, sir, Mr. President."

"Now, business."

"My first plan is to build a safe haven city in Texas near the border, to help immigrants work and live while waiting for citizenship. If anyone thinks this is a bad idea, speak up now."

Darien looked around. "Second, Mr. Vice President, I would like you to negotiate with the new Russian president and Ukraine to ensure no wars start up again. Third, Lieutenant, I need you to strategize a plan to eliminate terrorism. Lina, you'll be my eyes and ears in the safe haven city. Terrell, I need you to recruit a safe haven city secret force. Rebecca, do a press release on the plan to build a safe haven border city. Mr. Edwin, can you get me an expert building project planner?"

"Sure, I think this is a good start. Thanks,"

"Mr. President, Mr. Edwin is here requesting to see you."

"Yes, Miss Pearl, send him in right away and give Mr. Edwin a VIP badge."

Edwin walked in.

"Have a seat, Mr. Edwin. Okay, what do you have?"

"I talked with the expert planner. We need a 225,000-acre area. They suggest Eagle Pass, Texas. It's not close to any major US city, so no American citizens will need to be relocated. They suggest building a military base around the safe haven city for security reasons. This area can support up to 1.5 million people in normal times and up to 2 million in emergencies. For living quarters, we'll need 4,000 20-story family unit complexes and 1,000 temporary 10-story studio dwelling units, with 80,000 acres for crops and facilities, etc. The estimated building cost is $12.2 billion."

Darien looked at Edwin. Edwin smiled, "Son, I know it's a lot, but this is America."

"Um, okay. How long to build?"

"Well, with expert skilled labor and skilled immigrant labor working 24/7, it could take 2 or 3 years. If you can get Texas Governor Dee to agree, it is state land."

Darien pressed the intercom. "Miss Pearl, get Governor Dee on call."

"Yes, sir. One moment, please."

"Hello, Mr. President, what can I do for you?"

"Yes, Governor. I have a plan to build a safe haven city in your state."

"Okay." Governor Dee had a smile in his voice.

"I need about 225,000 acres of land in Eagle Pass, near the Mexico border. This safe haven city will be for immigrants coming to America to live and work while waiting for citizenship."

"Wait. Okay, Mr. President, you're saying to give immigrants American taxpayer dollars, land, and house them too? With all due respect, I can't agree. That's insane."

Darien's jaw clenched, and his scalp prickled. "Okay, Governor Dee. America works as a team, but you seem to think you're special. I'm the president for the people. If you can't agree, you can choose to find another job. I don't have time for selfish, corrupt governors thinking they deserve more than everyone else. Get on board or get out, Governor."

"You can't do this to me!"

Darien hung up before he finished.

Edwin stared at Darien, thinking to himself, "President Thomas." Darien looked up and saw Edwin staring at him.

"Calming down, I'm sorry, Edwin."

"No, son, it's okay. For a moment, I saw your old man. Listen, I'm going to lunch. Are you hungry?"

"Um, yes, I can use a break."

"Okay, I know just the place."

Lieutenant Antonio left the meeting, thinking about the new president's request to finally stop terrorism in its tracks. This is what his special ops team was created for. He went back to his office to call the ops team for a meeting.

"Guys, I would like everyone to meet me in the ops planning room at 0800 Monday morning," he hung up and thought, "I will need all hands on deck for this one."

Leaving the White House, he got into his armored electric jeep and reached over to pull out his black book, a former military contract list. He hoped some were still alive. He started calling, and by the time he arrived home, he found five still living, thinking that was enough.

"These are true out-of-the-box planners. I might not always agree with these guys tactically, but when it comes to tactical planning, they are the best I know."

Sitting in his jeep in the driveway, he saw two dogs peeing on his flowers. He grabbed his military paintball gun from special ops maneuvers and snapped into combat mode, moving seamlessly. He opened the door quickly, drawing his gun before the dogs realized he was aiming at them and could escape. He shot both in the snout, and the dogs howled, rolling in the lawn grass trying to get the red paint off. Antonio felt sorry for them, but he really loved those flowers. The dogs, still worrying about the paint on their snouts, didn't run, looking at him as if, "We can take this guy."

Antonio smiled, giving them credit for having guts, then blasted them five more times with the paintball gun, making them realize this was not the place or time to stand around. Howling, they ran off. Lieutenant felt better about his flowers, replaced the paintball gun, and went inside, never letting his guard down, an ingrained habit from the military. He disarmed booby traps and cleared every room before finishing up by making a pot of coffee. Then, after taking a quick shower, he came out to find the coffee ready, grabbed a cup, and went to the back patio table to sit down.

He took in the beauty of the flowers, smelling the fragrant jasmine and nightingale, the only scents in the city that reminded him of his cabin in the forest. Relaxing, he fell into tactical planning mode, very still yet steering straight ahead, aware of every surrounding as he began planning the demise of terrorism.

"First, this enemy has no fear. Second, this enemy can't be reasoned with. Third, the enemy thrives on fear. Now, let's reward military and citizens who help capture terrorists. Second, put out bounties on individual terrorists. Third, mix evil with evil and let evil kill itself."

Taking a break, he got up and went inside to grab more coffee and make a phone call.

"Hello, is this NASA's chief engineer?"

"This is Lieutenant."

"Yes, sir, Lieutenant, I remember you. What can I do for you?"

"Is it possible to build an undersea prison with the capacity for one million inmates? Second, automated robots to run the facility, keeping order and capable of self-defense without weapons to prevent intrusion. Third, a seawater transfer system that can flood sections to force sabotager out. Fourth, small enough ventilation systems to make escape impossible."

"Yes, I think we can engineer this."

"Okay, make this top priority."

"Any requests about this project are to come to me or the president only."

"Yes, sir."

"Cost will not be a problem. Can you have blueprints and a small mock-up ready for demonstration in three weeks?"

"Yes, sir,"

Lieutenant hung up, noticing five missed calls. He returned encrypted group calls to his comrades.

"Hey guys, I need your help with plans to finally stop terrorism in its tracks."

"What? Is that possible?"

"Maybe not, but guys, are you willing to help slow it down?"

"Well, I'm doing nothing here but field dressing my wife's colt 22. Yeah, I'll help." The others laughed.

"I'm bored to death watching this bull crap news about other countries bad-mouthing America. Yes, I will help."

"I'm ready for some real action."

"Okay, guys, I will send military retrieval to bring you guys to Area 51, where we can plan the project demise seabed."

"Hey, why that name?"

"I will explain when we meet. Two guys are missing."

"Don't worry, I can find them. Those two live off-grid."

"Okay, thanks guys."

The next morning, Lieutenant Antonio met with his special ops team.

"Okay, guys, the president requested we draw up a plan to eliminate terrorism."

His teammates started laughing. "We've been trying for 20 years to stop terrorism; this is impossible."

Lieutenant Antonio fixed his gaze on the laughing soldier with true anger. They had never seen him angry before. The laughter immediately stopped, replaced by real fear. "Never say it's impossible. That disrespects our fellow soldiers who gave their lives to do the impossible."

After a tense 45 seconds, he broke his stare. "Okay, guys, this is what the special ops team was created for. I've called in some old comrades to help with this one. We'll all meet in Area 51 to plan tactical scenarios. You're all getting the weekend off. Enjoy it, because you'll be deployed for six months or however long it takes to get the job done. Dismiss."

At Area 51, Lieutenant walked in and greeted the gentlemen. "Comrades, thank you for coming. I won't waste time getting to the point. The president requested we stop terrorism once and for all. I know this is a hard request, but this is what we do. If it were easy, we wouldn't be here. Now, give me your ideas."

Twenty-four hours later, they had a workable tactic for flushing, capturing, and killing terrorists. "Okay, this may work," Lieutenant Antonio nodded. "Before I arrived, I called NASA engineers to plan and construct a terrorism sea bed prison. That's why this project is named 'Demise Sea Bed.'"

The comrades smiled, seeing the potential in the underwater prison.

"Okay, ops team and comrades, we'll all work on this project until we've filled this prison to capacity."

"How big is this prison? There are a lot of terrorists."

"It will hold one million prisoners."

"Wow, you really plan to pull weeds."

"That's the plan," Lieutenant smiled.

"All in," the comrades were in unison.

"Okay, ops team, get me a list of all known terrorists."

He flew back to Washington to discuss the plan with the president.

President Darien nodded as Lieutenant Antonio presented the plans. "Okay, Lieutenant, I like it. Make it happen."

"Miss Pearl, have Rebecca come to my office."

"Yes, Mr. President." Fifteen minutes later, Rebecca arrived.

"I need you to make an announcement to the nation about these two new projects and the budget allocated costs."

"Project 1 is a new safe haven city, estimated cost 12.2 billion, redirected from Ukraine aid to eliminate illegal border crossings and help those who just want peace and opportunity. Project 2 is an underwater facility for holding international terrorists and high-risk criminals, estimated cost 35.6 billion, to rid the nation of oppression and homegrown corruption."

One week later, President Darien's approval rating rose to 90%. News reports highlighted the first time American opinion was truly changed by a promise kept, giving America's people purpose and hope. The new border safe haven city solution solved border issues and created jobs, giving hope to all of humanity.

After seeing the news report, Governor Dee called. "Mr. President, Governor Dee is on the phone, requesting to speak with you, sir."

"Okay, send his call through."

"Mr. President, I think you've made a big mistake. You're letting these immigrants take advantage of America. We worked hard to build this country, and you're just letting these people in. They will degrade this country."

"Are you American?"

"Yes."

"Okay, what does America stand for?"

"What? Uh... That's it," Governor Dee stumbled.

"Exactly. You don't know. You think because you were here first, you have more rights."

"Yes, why not?"

"Wrong. The Creator gave you this privilege, and you just lost it."

"What?!"

"Governor Dee, you're no longer the Texas governor. Please vacate the office by Monday or be arrested for disobeying a presidential direct order."

"What? You can't do this."

President Darien smiled. "Well, I heard you have to step on some people to lead. Goodbye, ex-governor."

Darien pressed the intercom, instructing Miss Pearl to ask Lina to come to his office.

"Yes, Mr. President."

Ten minutes later, Lina arrived.

"Mr. President, you asked to see me?"

"Yes, have a seat. How are things in the safe haven city?"

"Well, everyone knows the rules. Anyone caught with drugs is automatically banned from living in the safe haven city and the country. Immigrants are happy and accept the rules. With the security, no crime has made it into the safe haven city yet, but we still have drugs coming across the border."

"Okay, I have a plan. I want to offer guaranteed citizenship for any immigrant who helps catch or identify drug smugglers crossing the border. I also plan to offer a $1,000 reward for any U.S. citizen for catching wanted drug smugglers, with a guaranteed pardon if the smuggler is injured while being captured. This $1,000 reward also applies to Mexican and Canadian citizens."

Lina smiled at Darien. "I like your idea."

"Lina, would you like to break this news to the nation?"

Lina looked up, staring at Darien for a moment in disbelief.

"Yes. It's your chance to fix America."

She left Darien's office giddy with pride.

"Miss Pearl, have Rebecca come to my office."

"Yes, Mr. President."

"Rebecca, have you had dinner yet?"

"No, sir, Mr. President."

"Good, let's go. We'll ride to dinner in the president's private limousine."

"Rebecca, I fired Governor Dee. I think he will try to cause problems. Here's what I would like you to do. Send some of your paparazzi to Texas to hound him and put him in the news spotlight. Every time he comes out in public, ask uncomfortable questions like, 'Why do you disagree with building the border safe haven city?'"

"Okay, can I include this in my press release?"

"These reporters will make him lose his hair," Darien laughed.

Rebecca kissed Darien. "I'm sorry, forgive me. I don't know what came over me."

"It's okay. I feel safe with you."

"Thank you."

Two years later, the safe haven city was completed, illegal border crossings reduced to zero, and drug smugglers were on the run from bands of citizen bounty hunters. News reporters were live at the U.S.-Mexico border, speaking with immigrants in tears, saying, "My most lucrative job and guaranteed way to become a U.S. citizen came from hunting the smugglers that used and abused me. I just want to say to the American president, muchas gracias, thank you, sir."

Chapter 10

Embracing The Legacy

"Mr. President, will you be going on vacation this year?"

"Yes, I will."

"Very good, sir.

"I would like to see the world."

"Okay, sir. Where to first?"

"No, I meant to see the planet from the International Space Station. Is this possible?"

"Yes, sir. Just unexpected. We can make it happen if you're sure."

"Yes, I am. A leader must see to understand the true privilege of his leadership, the responsibility he has in charge to care for."

One month later, NASA finishes arranging the president's trip to the International Space Station.

Darien smiled. "Rebecca, how would you like to go with me?"

"Oh, no, Mr. President. I'm afraid of heights, sorry. But I can let the nation know where you are and how brave you are."

Rebecca, smiling, gave Darien a hug. "I'll be here when you return."

"Lieutenant, I'm ready."

"Yes, sir, this way."

Darien's spaceship takes off without any problem. The space ship's G force makes Darien realize the power he's been granted. Nine minutes later, he's in space, feeling weightless. He looked out the spaceship window back at planet Earth, seeing its true power and beauty. Speechless, there were no words, only emotions: awe, joyousness, peace, wonder, pleasure, fear, respect. Darien, in a trance, watched the Earth float on nothingness, thinking, "How is this possible?"

Once Darien reached the space station, for the entire two-week vacation, he watched at the planet Earth, the blues, purples, greens, yellows, reds. Thinking to himself, "The creator is real. I must use the power given to me to save this invaluable planet. Now I know why my father and Jonathan tried so hard. It's worth dying for."

Darien returned to Earth determined to make a change to help take care of this gift, feeling a new understanding when he landed. He knew his place in the cosmos. After arriving back at the White House, he spoke briefly to the public about making visits to the International Space Station a requirement for all presidents.

Darien gets a call from climate control scientist. "Mr. President, this is Chelsea from the Climate Scientist Tracking Agency. The planet's warming markers of 0.2% have been reached. We have one year to slow climate warming, or planet Earth will copy Venus' atmosphere. Once the temperature reaches 0.3%, there is nothing we can do to stop global warming. At that point, all life will need to be moved to another planet or burn to death."

"Are you sure?"

"Yes, Mr. President. I've been working on this for 20 years. I love planet Earth. I don't want to lose it or leave."

"Okay, thanks, Chelsea." He hangs up.

Darien sat alone in the Oval Office's private sitting room, thinking to himself. "Creator, I know you can hear my thoughts. I believe you gave me all this power for a reason. How can I help your people? You gave me the Book of Truth" He remembered his father's words to Jonathan, "Son, don't ask 'What can I do?' Look inside; He's there. Be patient; He will answer." Looking inward, he's thinking, "What should I do?"

Rebecca calls Darien. "Yes, I'm in the sitting room."

"Darien, are you okay? I heard you talking in the dark I forgot to give you this." She placed a gift on the table and came over, sitting down beside him, gazing into his eyes. "Darien, there is an aura of power around you, like a flame." Not knowing how to say what's really on her mind, she walked over to open the bay window curtain, revealing the full moon. Rebecca's shadow was across the private sitting room and seemed to flicker, separating and falling to the floor.

Darien was in a dreamlike trance when he heard glass breaking and Rebecca gasping for breath. He jumped up, catching her, screaming in his mind, "No, not her!" His knee touched the floor, Lieutenant Antonio's special ops team was on the shooter. Terrell's Secret Service agents and paramedics, following close behind, rushed in. "I'm here, brother." Terrell shouted, as Darien, dazed and with watering eyes.

"Is she alive?"

"Barely." The paramedics rushed Rebecca to the hospital.

"Mr. President, are you okay?"

"Yes, bring me the shooter now."

When Antonio arrived with the shooter in handcuffs, a loud thunder shook the window panes. "Governor Dee, why?"

"I worked hard for this country, and you let these immigrants run in like rats." Darien's eyes flashed, his jaw clenched, and in a blinding flash, ex-Governor Dee's eyes rolled back as blood dripped from his nose, falling to the floor. Even Antonio didn't see Darien strike ex-Governor Dee.

"Get this scum out of my sight."

Darien turned to Lieutenant Antonio, gripping his arm tightly. "I will have no pity on people who kill innocent people because they cannot have their way. Promise me they won't know another day of rest, only nightmares. This must stop."

The intercom rings.

"Yes, Miss Pearl?"

"It's the hospital."

"Put them through."

"Hello, Doc. Will she live?"

"Yes. The bullet went through muscle, collarbone, and shoulder blade."

"Okay, thanks, Doc."

"I need to be alone."

Terrell moved everyone out.

"You got it."

Darien saw a crushed potted plant on the floor. He picked it up. He didn't recognize the plant and saw the tag label: fig tree. He thought about Rebecca's gift and started laughing with tears, thinking to himself, "That's it. Let's grow some food and feed the hungry."

Darien disappeared into a secret room to consult the Book of Truth.

Sitting in the secret Oval Office room, Darien turned the Book of Truth over. Concentrating, words began to appear: "Convert entire state into hydroponic greenhouses to increase food sources while reducing water use. Dedicate 10% of the country's land to forest. Convert entire state to farmland for livestock." As the words disappeared, Darien thought, "How can I get people to relocate to save the plants from climate catastrophe?"

Putting the Book of Truth back in the safe, he remembered the Book of Ideology. Smiling, he left and called a meeting with America's top scientists.

"Gentlemen, you are here because I have been advised we are reaching the point of no return with climate control." One of the scientists started murmuring about whether it was true or not.

"Gentlemen, we don't have time for debates, and frankly, I don't care. We will try to save this planet. I didn't invite you here

115

to ask. I'm executing presidential authority. You will work on the project I assign."

"We have rights; you can't force us."

"Are you refusing a presidential order?"

"No, I'm just saying—"

"Lieutenant, lock this guy up until we get this climate problem under control."

"Yes, sir."

"But you can't do this—" The Secret Service snatched the scientist out of the room.

Darien looked around. "Anyone else want to waste my time?" No one spoke.

"Now, I have three projects. I need speed, quality, and 110% priority and effort. Any questions?"

"Okay, gentlemen, let's save this planet. It's all we got."

Darien gave a press release to the nation about the climate threat to humanity. "This is our only home.". With the Book of Ideology, he passed laws making the entire state of Arizona a hydroponic greenhouse state, declaring the entire state of Louisiana a farm state for livestock, and declaring Minnesota, Oklahoma, and Missouri as nature tree forest states to improve atmospheric pollution levels. Business was illegal in these states except for roadway and forest-keeping facilities. All three laws passed unanimously.

As Darien's success grew, other nations took notice of America's reaction to the president's innovations in climate control and economic stimulation. The Queen of England visited Darien, asking for his advice on improving her country's relations and productivity. The day before the Queen's arrival, Darien consulted the Book of Truth, which showed him the questions she would ask. Darien answered all her questions. The Queen was impressed with his answers and ideas so much that she immediately passed similar

116

laws in her country, declaring hydroponic greenhouse states, livestock farms, and tree forest states.

As Darien's ideas spread, the Book of Ideology was needed less and less. Allied countries adopted economic and forest projects to help reduce climate and migration problems. However, other countries with stricter ideologies were not willing to change and made plans to interfere. President Mai Cha Lee of China, aware of the Book of Ideology's existence, sent an ambassador delegation to spy and search for America's weaknesses.

Darien, suspicious, consulted the Book of Truth, which revealed President Mai Cha Lee's search for the Book of Ideology. The next morning, Darien called Lieutenant Antonio. "I need you to show China that when a country looks weak, it's not always true."

Antonio called Conrad and the special ops team for a meeting. "The president requests we demonstrate to Mai Cha Lee that Americans don't start wars, but looks can be deceiving. It might be easier to swallow a camel than to fight a war against America."

Special Ops leader Ider smiled eagerly, ready to test America's new military tools. "Okay, Conrad, you come along and observe why we're called Ghost Nightmare."

"Okay, Ops team, Monday, 6:30 AM at China's coastline."

China's President Mai Cha Lee got a call from his military commander. "Sir, the Americans are here."

"What are you talking about?"

"The entire coastline. No one can see anything, but our radar suddenly picked up 500 warships and 250 military submarines sitting one mile offshore."

"Impossible!"

"You're telling me you did not see the warships approaching?"

"No. The radars gave no warning. There must be a Malfunction sir."

"Where did the fog come from?"

"Don't know, sir. It seems as if the fog hid them from radar sensors."

"Okay, Ider, retract the fog."

"Yes, sir."

Lieutenant called the Darkstar fighter jets squadron to perform a low flyover with sonic booms at Mai Cha Lee's palace in two minutes. "Okay, Mr. President, squadron standby."

Darien called China's President Mai Cha Lee. "Hold on, Commander. I'm getting a call from the American president now."

"Hello, Mr. Mai Cha Lee, this is Darien. I've made this as plain as possible. You think American hospitality is your hotel, and you can come in and be disrespectful without paying. Well, think of me as the concierge, delivering notice of the bill due. And if your delegation stays too long, that collection agency sitting off your coast is to make sure the bill gets paid. You have a nice day, Mr. President."

As Mai Cha Lee's phone clicked off, a tremendous sonic boom shook the building as 15 Darkstar fighter jets traveling at Mach 6 passed over Mai Cha Lee's palace. This went on for five seconds, one after another, traveling so fast that Mai Cha Lee saw no jets, only heard sonic booms as the building shook. Picking up the phone, he recalled the delegation immediately.

Then, the fog cleared. What the China commander saw made his blood run cold: a massive convoy of military warships and submarines that no nation could hide, some so futuristic he couldn't identify, bristling with so many weapons.

The commander turned to his second in command. "Go to the mess hall, bring that whiskey bottle. I need a drink."

"Ider, fog us. We're done here."

"Yes, sir."

Ider activated the stealth fogger. The China commander watched as the fog returned, taking another swallow of whiskey. He turned to the radar; the blob indicating American ships disappeared. In 15 minutes, the fog dissipated, and the commander looked out toward the ocean, but all 500 warships and submarines had disappeared. The military's ghost stealth radar fog worked perfectly, enabling warships to submerge unseen. American science engineers invented sub-warships that could submerge to travel unseen.

One month later, a terrorist attack in Israel killed 500 Israelis. The Israeli Prime Minister called the American President for help.

"Mr. President, you have a call from the Israeli Prime Minister."

"Thank you, Miss Pearl. Put him through."

"Hello, Ya Seen Dai, how are you?"

"I'm well, Mr. President, but I have a problem. Terrorists attacked last night, killing 500 Israeli citizens and demanding we leave the West Bank. We need your help to stop these Terrorists."

"Okay, Ya Seen Dai. I will send you my Ghost Ops team." The President hung up the phone.

"Call Lieutenant."

"Yes, sir." entering the office.

"Mr. President." Lieutenant stepped in the room.

"How is your plan for stopping terrorists coming along?"

"We have plans, just need your permission to test them."

"Well, Lieutenant, I just received a call from Israeli Prime Minister Ya Seen Dai. He needs help. Terrorists killed 500 Israeli citizens last night. I'm sending you to eliminate or capture them— you decide. Just make sure you send a hard message that terrorists will no longer be tolerated."

"Yes, sir." The lieutenant left the office and returned to his own. He sat down, leaning back in his chair, contemplating the President's emphasis on sending a particularly hard message to terrorists. "What can make an evil person have nightmares?" Antonio goes home to think deeply about it.

Upon arriving home, he pulled into the driveway and noticed the flowers blooming. "Good, those dogs understand these flowers are off limits." He was always aware of his surroundings. He approached the door and noticed the thread on the doorknob was broken. Without moving his head, he looked left and right, checking if an intruder was still nearby. Deactivating the booby trap, he went inside, checked all the traps, and then returned to the surveillance monitor. He saw a slim figure dressed in black, wearing a ski mask, touching the doorknob and looking up at the mini cam, then back down at the broken thread. The figure backed away, head down, and disappeared into the darkness. After checking all cameras and seeing no further activity, Antonio went to fix the special trap for this unwanted guest.

After fixing the booby trap, ensuring the thief would never forget, Antonio called his Ops team. "We have another mission, and this one involves terrorists."

"Where at?"

"Israel. The President wants to send an extreme message."

"Ider, let the whole team know we're deploying to Israel in one week."

"Yes, sir."

"And ready the military ghost terminator robots."

"But, sir, the last time they ripped arms and legs off targets. That's why the project was shut down."

"I know, but the President wants an extreme message sent. We will execute the original plan on this mission."

"Yes, sir." He hung up. Antonio then called Conrad. "Hey, we have a terrorist mission in Israel. I would like you to come along."

"Yes, count us in."

"Intelligence says there are about 143 terrorists involved in killing 500 citizens. We deploy one week from now."

Antonio called a NASA engineer.

"Hello, Lieutenant. What do you need?"

"Human tamper-proof neck collars, able to deliver extreme pain when tampered with, and also a location tracker."

"Wait, wait, Lieutenant, this seems like torture."

"I thought you might feel that way. Did you watch the news about the terrorist attack in Israel?"

"Yes."

"These collars are for those guys."

"Now you have my attention. Say no more. I will make this a top priority. I had a friend get killed in that attack."

"I need this in one week."

"Okay, I will have them ready."

"Make sure the collars work."

"Yes, sir. You have my word on this."

One week later, at 0300, the deployment in Israel began.

"Lieutenant, we've located the terrorist hideout."

"Okay, Ider. Activate the ghost fog."

"Yes, sir."

Two hours later, the entire city was shrouded in fog.

"Upload terminator robots with target facial recognition information. Give each robot five targets."

"Sir, that means only 18 will survive."

"Yes, I know. It's a bad day to be a terrorist. Okay, Ops team, 18 terrorists are not marked for destruction. Get in, capture the targets, and get out. Any questions?"

No one spoke.

"Okay, don't embarrass me by getting shot."

"Yes, sir."

Antonio looked at each Ops team member, sensing no fear "Let's get it done. I need 18 collared terrorists."

Ider activated the terminator robots first. One Ops team member jumped up, slamming his hand down on the button to open the door.

"Ider, remember what happened the last time you activated before opening the door."

"Oh man, yeah, they ripped the door and part of the ship wall to get out. I forgot. Thanks."

"The lieutenant was so mad he ripped my favorite shades off and crushed them." The team laughed.

"Where'd you get the new shades? Walmart?"

"Yeah, how did you know?" He looked around to make sure the lieutenant wasn't close by, then whispered, "The first ones cost me $450."

Ider looked back to the terminator monitor and heard a man scream, "No, please!" followed by howling in pain.

"Go now, before the robots destroy all the targets."

The Ops team headed out, hearing screams, dogs barking, gunfire, and pleas for mercy. Then came the sounds of unbearable pain: "Oh God, please, my legs! No, oh Jesus, my arm!"

"What are you?" The terminator robot didn't speak. The terrorist held up his hand in defense. The robot moved extremely quick and grabbed the arm at elbow and snatched it. The terrorist's mouth opened to scream, but no sound came out. The pain was too much. He felt wetness and extreme heat on his face, as if he were too close to a red-hot stove. He struggled to process the pain, hoping his mind would shut down, but it didn't. All he could think was nightmare and flickering images of hell before darkness overtook him.

The Ops team captured 18 terrorists after eliminating malfunctioning robots. The team radioed in, "Ider, order the robots back to the extraction point and send a retrieval unit for the malfunctioning robots."

"Copy. Lieutenant, we have 18 living terrorists, returning now."

"Good job, gentlemen."

After returning from the Israel mission, Lieutenant Antonio informed the President in detail about the actions taken to send a message. Darien, after hearing the lieutenant's report, reminded himself to be more careful with such requests. Feeling remorse but accepting the consequences in order to deter future aggression.

"Very good, Lieutenant. You may leave." As Antonio left the President's office, he sensed the President's hesitation about violence but accepted the necessity.

Rebecca awoke in the hospital, feeling disoriented and in pain. Her shoulder was in extreme pain. She remembered hearing glass breaking, feeling a white-hot pain, and then hearing Darien screaming before everything went black. As she turned her head, she saw a TV reporting live news about Israel 2 weeks ago..

500 Israeli citizens were tragically massacred by a terrorist group. The Israeli Prime Minister, Ya Seen Dai, had called the American President for help. Last night, Israeli citizens witnessed a thick fog covering the entire city around 3 AM. Sounds of men screaming, dogs barking, and machine gun fire were heard. An hour later, the fog disappeared, and Israeli police discovered 125 bodies with heads, arms, and legs torn off. All the bodies were identified as terrorists.

The report then shifted focus, mentioning Rebecca. The news detailed how a White House press reporter was shot while in the President's private sitting room. The Secret Service and a special ops team apprehended the shooter, identified as Governor Dee of Texas. Sources stated that the governor disagreed with the President's Safe Haven City project in his state and was upset about the incoming immigrants, which he believed was destroying the American way of life. In his anger, he attempted to kill the President.

President Darien released a statement in response: "I understand Americans' feelings about drugs and violence pouring in across the border. I will address this problem, but one person killing another because he can't have his way is wrong. People, let's work together and show the rest of the world why we are called Americans. Thank you."

As Darien left the press room, a reporter shouted, "Why should we help these immigrants who are killing us with drugs?" Darien stopped and turned around. "Did your mother and father help you when you were wrong?"

"Yes."

"And did you learn anything from that?"

The reporter sat down.

"The Creator made America to be a mother and father to all humanity. If you don't want to be American, you can leave."

Two months later, Rebecca returned to her job as the White House Press Secretary. Darien, glad to have her back, invited her to his office to see how she was doing. When she noticed the fig tree she had given him growing beautifully, she smiled, feeling happy and appreciated.

Later that evening, Darien went to his secret room to consult the Book of Truth about drugs and gang violence. The book revealed: fortify every city for all proven honest working citizens with military peacekeeping forces, create a bounty hunter program giving citizens permits to hunt drug dealers for rewards, and form militia groups to protect rural areas. Once again, the words disappeared. Darien felt a presence behind him but did not turn around. Suddenly, he heard in his mind, "My son." Overwhelmed by fear and then understanding, Darien thought in his mind, "Thank you." Leaving the secret room, he walked into the White House forest, a beautiful area planted with trees and flowers extending for a square mile in every direction, a part of the climate control project.

NASA contacted Lieutenant Antonio.

"Hello, sir."

They informed him him they had the plans ready for the undersea prison he had requested.

"If you can stop by, we can discuss the plans in details." The engineer explained the building logistics and cost estimates. Antonio then discussed these details with President Darien, focusing on how the prison would pay for itself over time. Darien presented the proposal to the American people, who overwhelmingly agreed to the project, which was estimated to take seven years to complete.

During the construction, the Ghost Opt Terminator robots were deployed, capturing 100,000 terrorists and destroying 250,000. "Mr. President, I think we've broken the terrorists. They no longer speak openly. They've gone underground, fearing capture or termination. Even communist countries don't rebel for fear of waking up in the fog."

Lina, reporting live from the border Safe Haven City, spoke with an immigrant named Rashad. "Why do you risk your life hunting drug smugglers?"

"I must protect my new home. It feels good to feed my family with the reward money. If I could, I would hunt drug smugglers to extinction. I think the American President is very wise. He creates jobs and stops crime at the same time. Thank you, Mr. President, for this opportunity."

The militia in rural areas were also interviewed. DJ, a member of the South Carolina militia brigade, explained how they kept gangs from taking over rural neighborhoods. "Every night, gangs try selling drugs and recruiting young children. But we post on walls, fence posts, and street signs with high rewards. When gang members see their pictures on wanted posters, they stay away for fear of being caught. Some we capture, but most stay away because of the sea prison."

One year later, President Darien's approval rating was 99%, ushering in the most stable economy in history. Peace, prosperity, a stable climate, and worldwide stability and understanding between humanity and the environment were achieved. Darien gave a speech to the nation: "People of America, I thank you for trusting me to lead America back to its place of honor and purpose. I mean to continue fighting evil in high places with loyalty to the people. But you have to choose between ideology and the truth because our enemies are waiting, looking for a weak spot."

In the crowd, a breathtakingly beautiful Chinese was staring at him. Darien blinked, losing his concentration, confused and bewildered. He cut his speech short. "Choose the truth, my fellow Americans. Thank you." As he left the podium, Rebecca asked, "What's wrong?

"Mai Cha Lee is back."

Made in the USA
Columbia, SC
08 November 2024

45791750R00072